A POLITICAL PROPOSAL

E. C. FOUNTAIN

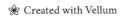

For my husband, who will forever be my miracle. I love you.

For Nene, who made me a lifelong reader.

For Mom and Dad, I'll never be able to repay you for all the things you've done. Thank you for always loving me.

A POLITICAL PROPOSAL

BY

E. C. FOUNTAIN

1

February 14, 2014

Lila Hudson wheeled the rented Crown Victoria into the Wisteria Inn parking lot. Slush flew as the tires sank into the rutted out parking spot. Lightning streaked across the sky, followed by a loud clap of thunder. *Great, just great.* She jumped out of the car, grabbed a small suitcase, and ran for it. She flung the door open, slamming it against the wall.

The receptionist jumped, then plastered on a shaky smile. "Welcome to the Wisteria Inn." The woman had to be pushing ninety years old. She'd probably given the elderly lady heart palpitations. Lila pushed her blond hair off her face, then gave the best smile she could muster given the situation.

"Hi, I'm Lila Hudson. I called a few hours ago for a room."

"Yes, ma'am. We've got it all ready for you." The receptionist turned to find the key. *Ma'am?* Maybe the events of the past few weeks had aged her. She'd never been called *ma'am* in her life.

"Here you go, dear. Your room is the first door on the left upstairs. 201."

"Thank you." Lila clutched the keys, shivering from the cold. *A hot shower. Everything will be better after a hot shower.* She turned to head up the stairs, then stopped. A piano played in the distance.

"Our restaurant with full bar is down the hall," said the receptionist. "We are having hot stew. Plus, our chef is making his famous chocolate cake with hot fudge and raspberries tonight for Valentine's Day."

Valentine's Day. She tried to avoid even thinking about that stupid holiday. "Bar? You serve alcohol here?" She'd quickly learned certain counties in the South didn't sell hard liquor. At this point, she was pretty sure she could get hammered off beer. Even nasty, cheap beer.

"Yes, ma'am. Our bartender makes a fine mint julep, if that suits your fancy."

Lila bit her tongue. It would take something a heck of a lot stronger than a mint julep to help her get some sleep tonight. "Thank you." She grabbed her bag, then climbed the stairs. She opened the door to Room 201, finding a quaint room filled with soft pastels and a magnolia scented candle burning on the bedside table. It smelled like heaven. The need for a shower overpowered the appeal of the bed. Which was overpowered by the need for a drink.

She glanced in the mirror. Her blond hair hung in sad, heavy locks to her shoulders. Mascara stained the skin beneath her eyes. She picked up the bar of soap next to the sink and washed her face, then combed her hair. *Not gonna win any beauty awards, but it will do.* She grabbed her purse, purposefully leaving her cellphone on the nightstand. For good measure, she reached over and turned the phone off.

Feeling better already, she grabbed her favorite red lipstick and swiped it across her mouth.

The small restaurant had cozy, old fashioned curtain booths allowing guests complete privacy. The waiter ducked in and out of the booths, moving like a discrete shadow. A tiny bell was attached to each station to ring the waiter. From what Lila could see, there may have only been one or two booths in use. *I'm sure this weather is keeping lovers at home and in bed tonight.* She pushed away the wave of sadness welling up in her chest.

There was only one other person sitting at the bar. The tall, well-built man with salt and pepper hair smiled at her, tipping his hand in a tiny salute. She smiled in spite of herself and chose a seat a few bar stools away from him. The bartender approached her, promoting his mint julep.

She didn't hesitate or consider any other offers. "Whiskey. On the rocks." Salt and pepper man smiled at her again, chuckling to himself. She almost didn't say anything, but the combination of the fatigue, loneliness, and anger that had been simmering for the past week compelled her.

"What are you laughing at?" Her pale blue eyes flashed hot.

"Whoa, no need to get hostile. I laughed because it looks like Gardner...that's our bartender friend...got shut down twice in a row on his mint juleps." He held up his glass. "Jack and Coke."

The anger eased back some. "Oh, ok. Sorry. Long week." Salt and pepper stood up and idled over to the seat beside her. *Geez, he's tall. Good looking, too.* She shook her head. *No time for that.*

"I'm Grant." He held out his hand.

"Lila." She slipped her small hand into his.

"Lila...That's a beautiful name." He smiled, lighting his whole face up. His dark eyes creased, giving him a worldly, kind air. He shook her hand. He continued to hold it, running his thumb across the top, sending goosebumps scattering across her arms. While his hair was sprinkled with gray, his eyebrows and eyelashes were coal black. There was stubble on his cheeks, silver mixing with black.

"I can't take credit. All my mother's doing." Gardener slid a drink to her. She released his hand and grabbed the drink. She willed her hand to stop shaking.

"Are you cold?" Grant placed his hand on her arm. Her long sleeve t-shirt was still damp from the rain. "You're soaking wet. Come on, let's get you by the fire."

She hadn't even noticed the small fireplace in the back of the restaurant, which was surrounded by a few overstuff rocking chairs. Grant placed a hand on her lower back, expertly guiding her. She sank down in the plush chair, surprised when tears filled her eyes. Caught unaware by the man's touch and kindness, the emotions from the week pushed up into her throat. She swallowed the tears down, willing herself to gain control.

"Thank you," she mumbled. He sat in the chair across from her, stretching his long legs out in front of him.

"You're welcome." He looked at her intently before flashing a grin. "So, tell me more about yourself, Lila."

"Just passing through. Flew into Miami from the Bahamas. Decided I wanted a road trip home."

"Where's home exactly?"

She hesitated. She didn't know this man. He could be an ax murderer. A handsome, kind, Southern ax murderer. She fished for a lie and settled for the truth. "D.C." His eyebrows lifted and something flashed across his face. He looked as if he was going to say something, then stopped.

"That's some road trip. I'm actually doing some traveling myself. Just local travel but sure have been spending a lot of time in the car. I'm from State College, about two hours from here."

"State College? What kind of name is that?"

"Exactly what it sounds like." He grinned at her. *He has perfect teeth*. Perfect size, perfect shape, blindingly white. *He has to get them bleached. No one has teeth that perfect.*

"You had braces, right?"

"Um, yes, I did." He frowned, puzzled.

"Your teeth. They are absolutely perfect."

"Good to know all those years of being called Bucky are long gone."

"Bucky?"

"You know, like buck toothed?"

Lila grimaced. "So, they were a sound investment?"

"Best money my parents ever spent." He bared his teeth again. Lila couldn't help but laugh.

"I had braces, too, thank God. Unfortunately, I looked rather similar to a horse in third grade."

"Well, nothing horsey about you now." Lila felt her guard rise up immediately. He seemed to sense the change in demeanor. "Have you had dinner yet? I was thinking about trying out the special. What do you think?" As if on cue, her stomach rumbled. She clutched a hand to her flat abdomen and smiled.

"I think that's a yes." Grant laughed and lifted his hand to signal the waiter. After ordering the stew and dessert, he informed Gardner to keep the drinks coming. "Tell me a little more about yourself."

She hesitated, trying to decide what to say to this good-looking stranger. *What the hell, I'll never see him again.*

"Well, like I said, I live in D.C. I teach psychology at Georgetown University."

"Psychology, huh? Pretty impressive. Are you going to psychoanalyze me tonight?"

Lila bit her lip to hold back a grin. "Maybe. Anything to hide?"

His chocolate brown eyes darkened, and he smiled a slow, easy grin. "Nothing that would interest you."

"I'll be the judge of that. After the last couple of weeks I've had, it'd be nice to hear about someone else's deep dark secrets."

"What happened in the past couple of weeks?"

Her pulse raced at the thought. "Let's just say it's been one for the record books. The Bahamas were supposed to be my getaway, but it wasn't all I'd hoped for. I mean, don't get me wrong, I like the beach, but I would have preferred going somewhere with more culture and history."

"Hmmm...maybe France?"

"That's a good choice. I'm dying to go to Ireland. Something about rolling hills and rain seems to call my name." She fiddled with the oval shaped emerald ring on her right hand.

"Why didn't you go there?" He looked at her like he was trying to read what lay beneath her comments.

"It's a long story. I already had tickets to the Bahamas, so I figured, why not use them?"

"Tickets? As in more than one? Did someone go with you?"

Her cheeks flushed. "No one. Just me." She offered a weak smile. "Enough about me, tell me a little more about you." Gardner slid another round of drinks in front of them without a word. Lila clutched the whiskey to her chest and stared up at the handsome man in front of her. Grant ran a hand through his hair, leaving the ends ruffled. The whiskey coursing through her veins had her resisting the urge to smooth his hair down.

"Not too much to tell. I've worked in State College for the city for several years and own an accounting firm. Been contemplating a job change, but who knows? Is it even worth the trouble?"

"I don't know." She shrugged. "All I've ever known is academia, I've never practiced psychology. I get by doing what I do, but it's not my passion." She twisted the emerald ring again. She didn't know if she'd ever said that out loud to anyone.

"So, what is your passion?"

The answer all but tumbled out of her mouth. "Painting." She felt a surge of energy pulse into her chest. "I've always loved to paint. It's one of the few times I feel peaceful. My mind wanders and settles onto whatever it wants. No pretending, no putting on a show, no trying to please everyone."

Understanding flashed in his eyes. "Maybe I should take up painting."

"That probably sounds crazy...It's just, well, it's just I always feel like I have to perform. Painting is something I do just for me."

Grant squeezed her hand, sending shock waves up her arm and down her spine. His dark eyes looked deep and soft, like an abyss of brown velvet. "I completely understand. I feel that way about writing. I keep a little notebook with me and jot down ideas when they pop in my head. Got four unfinished manuscripts collecting dust, but can never bring myself to finish one." He picked up the fresh drink Gardner placed in front of them and clinked glasses with her. Lila was losing track. *Was this drink number three or four? Surely not, five?*

"Why haven't you finished them?"

Grant wrung his hands. Instinctively, Lila reached out and stilled his hand with her own. He laced his fingers through hers as if it were the most natural thing in the world. Like they'd done it a thousand times. His thumb stroked her hand again. Her head roared, and heat filled her body.

"I don't know. I guess, because they're not perfect. It'd take so much work to get them turned into a real book someone would actually want to read that I stop and start something new." Lila tried to focus on her reply but all she could think about was his thumb rhythmically running over her hand. That sneaky ass Gardner slipped in again, slyly removing their empty glasses and placing another round of drinks in front of them without a word. The whiskey went down warm and smooth. At this point, there wasn't even a burn to it anymore.

"It sounds to me you are scared of what others will think. I get it. I'm the same way about my art. My mother called one of my paintings 'elementary.' That was the last time I let her see anything I painted. Now, as soon as I'm done, the paintings either go to Goodwill, or I hide my favorites in a closet."

"Sounds like your mother can be a bit of an ass." Grant's eyes widened. "I'm sorry. I don't even know your mother." She knew she should be irritated by the comment, but all she could do was laugh.

"No, you're right. She can be an ass." She looked over her shoulder, half expecting her mother to be there when she turned around. "I love her. And don't get me wrong, I know she loves me. She just...well, she just cares a lot about appearances. Wants everything to look perfect, everyone to be perfect." She glanced down at her French manicure and resisted the urge to bite her nails. "She just wears me out sometimes."

"Don't worry, you aren't the only one. At least your mother stayed around." Grant's face turned serious for a moment, but as quick as it clouded over, it cleared. The piano, which had been quiet for about an hour, picked back up. Thunder crashed outside, and the lights flickered. "Want to dance?" She nodded. He stood, then pulled her to her feet.

Lila swayed, feeling the rush from the booze when she

stood up. She gripped his arm, surprised at the lean muscle under his shirt. He smelled like sandalwood and something citrus. She allowed him to draw her closer, wrapping her arms around his neck. She breathed him in, feeling stubble brush against her forehead. His strong arms held her tight, and he softly ran a hand down to her lower back.

The song was a sad, melancholy tune that brought tears to her eyes. She didn't know why she felt the urge to cry, other than maybe the fact her entire life had come crashing down around her. Her face flushed with shame. *Focus on this moment, this man.* When she cleared her mind, all she could think of was his warm touch and the yearning welling up inside her.

Grant looked down at her. If he noticed the tears, he didn't say anything, but instead, cupped her face with his hand. His mouth was only a few inches from hers. Without waiting on him, Lila pulled him close, pressing her mouth to his. Grant mumbled something she couldn't understand and slipped his hand beneath her shirt to stroke the skin at the base of her spine. As his mouth expertly caressed hers, she felt as if everything from the past few horrible weeks was starting to fade away.

"Come up to my room," she murmured.

He didn't reply, only smiled. He walked to the bar, quickly paying their tab. He looked up at her, his dark eyes sparkling. Butterflies danced in her belly. Her heart pounded in her chest. He approached her, holding out his hand. She slipped her hand into his, and they laced their fingers together. They made it to the stairwell, before she pushed him against the wall.

She kissed his lips greedily, breathing in his scent. She tasted the hint of alcohol on his tongue. He held her tightly against him, her hips against his. He trailed kisses across her cheekbone into her hair. She pulled him closer, fighting the urge to moan.

When they finally reached the door, he pushed her against the door, still kissing her. The cold doorknob pressed into her back. She fumbled for the key, unsuccessfully trying to fit it into the lock. Grant covered her hand, sliding the key smoothly into place.

She felt breathless as Grant laid her on the bed. She pulled him closer, ripping a button off his shirt. He wrapped her blond hair around his hand, gently pulling her head back to expose her throat. Heat engulfed her body, as his mouth traveled from her mouth, down her neck, then wandered lower. He lifted her shirt, exposing creamy skin and lace. He stopped only long enough to pull a small foil packet from his wallet. With a grin, she pulled him back to her. The scent of magnolias still filled the room, as she allowed herself to give in to desire.

2

Sunlight poured into the quaint room, casting its beams on Lila's face. She covered her eyes, but the light beckoned her to face the day. When she finally brought herself to open her eyes, she was greeted by the blindingly white light streaming through the window. She jumped up to pull the curtains tight, stopping short when she realized she was completely naked. For a moment, she'd forgotten.

She covered her chest instinctively. *Grant.* He was lying face down, his bottom barely covered by the colorful quilt. Stealing a glance in the mirror, she reeled at the sight of herself. Her hair was mussed in the back, and dark circles rimmed her eyes. She tiptoed around the bed, gingerly picking up her toiletry bag and creeping into the bathroom.

She surveyed the damage, running a hand through mussed, oily hair. *Yikes.* She spritzed a few quick sprays of dry shampoo, then washed her face. She brushed her teeth and swiped on some deodorant. She turned to leave, then spritzed on some of her favorite Gucci perfume. Just for good measure.

Grant was still asleep, breathing deeply. She slid back

under the crisp sheets, smiling when he slung his arm over her, pulling her close to him. Unlike her, he looked as fresh this morning as he did last night. *Hot guys get morning breath, too, right?* She frowned, trying to decide if she wanted to find out. She pushed his hair back from his face.

His eyes blinked open. He smiled, looking mighty proud of himself, and kissed her on the nose. "Morning."

She smiled back, giving him a peck on the lips. "Good morning."

He curled around her, wrapping his leg over hers. "You smell good." *Thank you, Gucci.*

She breathed in his masculine scent, still smelling a hint of sandalwood. "Sleep ok?"

"Just perfect." He ran a hand down her arm. They both laid there quietly, until an alarm screeched on the bedside table. Grant reached over to silence it, then sat straight up. "What time is it?" Before she could answer, he grabbed his phone. "Oh, no." He jumped up. "Lila, I'm sorry. I've got to go. I completely forgot…" His voice trailed off, as he threw on his clothes. He jotted something down on the notepad sitting on the bedside table. As he struggled to button his shirt evenly, he gave up and leaned over to kiss her.

"Last night was amazing. I'm sorry I've got to leave like this but I have an appointment." He glanced at the clock. "Which I'm about to be late for." He pushed the paper at her. "Call me, ok?" He kissed her one more time, then was gone.

She looked down to see his phone number scribbled across the page. She'd wanted a rosy morning after, but maybe this was for the best. *Shower and coffee. In that order.*

She showered quickly, knowing the sooner she got done showering, the sooner she could get coffee. She used a cotton ball to apply toner to her face, then tossed it in the bathroom garbage. It landed softly on top of the condom from the night before. *Thank God.* She'd vaguely remembered him pulling the condom out of his wallet, but it calmed her to see confirmation staring back at her.

She dressed hurriedly, pulling on a pair of tight black jeans and a turquoise tunic. She jumped at the sound of her phone vibrating. *Mother.* Lila rolled her eyes and hit decline. Almost as soon as it stilled, the vibrating started up again. Sighing, Lila decided it was best to just get it over with.

"Hello."

"Lila? I've been worried sick about you. You didn't fly back in and no one knew where you were…Your father and I were almost ready to report you as a missing person!"

"Don't be dramatic, Mother. I'm fine. Just taking my time getting back home. I'm sure you and Dad weren't so much worried about me as much as you were worried about what others are saying about me."

"Lila Marie, don't you use that tone with me. We're worried about you. With Kent and all…well, we just didn't know what you'd do."

"Don't flatter Kent that much. I could think of far better things to do with my time than getting all hysterical over him."

"Lila, I know you've had a shock…"

"A shock? A shock? Well, yes, if you can call being left at the altar in front of five hundred of your nearest and dearest shocking, then yes, I'd say I was shocked."

"Lila," her mother started, but Lila interrupted her.

"I'm sorry for any harm this has done to you or Dad's image. I hate to disappoint you, but maybe someone in this family isn't perfect." Hot tears filled her eyes. She squeezed them shut, pushing the rage and shame down.

"Now, I know what Kent did was a little surprising…"

"Surprising? You call leaving me at the altar after he told me he loved me and wanted to spend his life with me surprising?" She let out a deep breath. "He never loved me,

Mother. Just wanted to use the good old family name to get ahead in life."

For once, Delores seemed to be at loss for words. "I don't know what happened, honey. He talked to your father and said something you said the night before scared him, and…"

"Scared him? All I did was tell him I was so glad we weren't going to be like you and Dad. That we actually loved one another and weren't just marrying to impress people. Guess I'm the one looking like a fool."

"Your father and I have a great deal of mutual affection and respect for one another, Lila. You'd do well to remember that."

"Yes, but I want love, Mother. Not mutual affection and respect."

"I'll have you know your father and I have built a wonderful life together on mutual affection and respect. Thirty-four years together and the envy of everyone in this town. So you watch your mouth, dear."

Lila sighed. They would never have the close mother and daughter relationship she longed for. "I'm sorry, Mother. I don't mean any disrespect. We just value different things."

"Well, maybe if you were a little more pleasant and not so abrasive, Kent would have stayed around. It's embarrassing, Lila. Your father's been dealing with this mess since you left."

And there it was. The whole point of this conversation. "I'll be home in the next week or so. I'm sure by that time Dad will have one of his cronies spin this story, somehow making it look like something other than his loser daughter being jilted at the altar."

Before her mother could say anything else, Lila hung up. She sat on the edge of the bed, stroking the pastel quilt. Images of Grant filled her mind. Grant holding her close, caressing her back with his big hands, kissing her mouth, smoothing her hair…She'd needed a man's touch. She'd needed to feel wanted, desirable, cared for. If only for one night. She remembered him kissing her goodnight and pulling her to him in the middle of the night.

Huge sobs racked her body, swallowing her in their rage. She'd made it ten days. Ten days after that horrible wedding without one tear, and the memory of Grant's touch broke her.

3

March 2014

I*'m having a stroke.* She couldn't move, couldn't speak. Her hand shook as she held the tiny stick in her hand that read "POSITIVE." She sat down to keep from falling. Her whole body was numb. *Isn't this what happens when you have a stroke?* She wiggled her toes experimentally. They moved, just like they were supposed to. *Maybe it's not a stroke. This can't be right. It just can't.* She looked at the test again and thought she might pass out. She laid her head back against the cold bathroom wall and forced herself to think.

It's probably just a false positive. We used protection. After a few more minutes of convincing herself it was just an error, she began to feel blood rush back to her brain. *Call Dr. Washington.* She grabbed her cellphone, searched her contacts, and finally, landed on the number for the gynecology clinic.

She stood up and began pacing around the bathroom. "Good afternoon, North Riverside OB-GYN Associates. This is Chevonne speaking. How may I help you?"

"Chevonne, yes, um…hi. My name is Lila Hudson. I need to speak to Dr. Washington."

"Dr. Washington is in clinic right now. I would be glad to get you to her nurse, Jennifer. Is this an emergency?" *Hell, yes, it's an emergency.* Lila tried to steady herself. She was Senator Hudson's daughter, for goodness' sake. She needed to hold it together. She wasn't dying. *Can't some tumors secrete pregnancy hormones? Maybe I have cancer?*

"Miss Hudson? Are you still there?"

"Yes, yes, I'm sorry. No, it's not an emergency."

"Ok, hold one moment, and I will send you to Jennifer's line." *Please pick up, please pick up.* The phone rang and rang. Jennifer's chirpy voicemail message asked her to please leave a message. Lila hung up the phone. Tears filled her eyes. She tried to calm herself, then called back.

"Good afternoon, North Lakeland OB-GYN Associates. This is Chevonne. How may I help you?"

"Chevonne, this is Lila Hudson. I, well, I do think this may be an emergency. Not a life or death emergency, but an emergency all the same." She could hardly finish before she burst into tears.

"Oh, honey, ok, hold on just a moment. I'm going to see if I can get someone to talk to you, ok? Hold on." It seemed like an eternity but, eventually, a brusque voice picked up.

"This is Mary, one of the nurses. How may I help you?"

"Yes, my name is Lila Hudson, and I just had a positive pregnancy test."

"Great. Hold on one second, and I'll transfer you to scheduling to get you set up for your first OB visit."

"Wait, wait…Please don't transfer me. You don't understand…I, uh, I…" Lila took a deep breath and tried to act like a normal human being. "I don't know if I'm really pregnant. God, I hope not. I was a few days late and took a test that came back positive." There was a pause on the other end before Mary spoke. This time, her voice was a little softer.

"Could you be pregnant, Miss Hudson?"

"No. Yes. God, I hope not. Oh my gosh…"

Mary raised her voice again. "Miss Hudson, take a deep breath." Lila breathed deeply. "Have you or have you not had sex since your last cycle?"

Lila's voice shook. "Yes, ma'am."

"We are open for a few more hours. If you come down here now, I'll get Dr. Washington to order a serum pregnancy test to let us know if you really are pregnant."

"Ok. I'm headed that way now." She breathed a sigh of relief. "Thank you, Mary."

"You're welcome." Lila hung up the phone. She grabbed her purse and raced out the door.

She slid into her car, ready to get to the clinic as soon as possible. She didn't know if she would know the results automatically or if it would take a day or two. Either way, the quicker she got there, the better. *Grant used protection.* The thought echoed in her mind. There was no way she was pregnant by her ex-fiancé. Kent had been out of the country on business the two months preceding the wedding. She'd thought it romantic to abstain until the wedding night, so they hadn't had sex when he arrived back home. She had two menstrual cycles during the time Kent was gone away on business.

She took a deep breath. *What if it was true? What if the condom failed?* She'd picked up her phone to call Grant several times since their night of passion but always chickened out. She'd felt an immediate physical and emotional connection to him, but after what she'd been through with Kent, she wasn't sure she could trust her judgement. Or her heart.

He probably forgot about me. I never even called. She gripped the steering wheel until her knuckles turned white. She hated to admit it was fear that had kept her from calling him. Her face blushed at the memory of his hands running over her body. *I didn't want to ruin the memory of that night.* She had debated and debated about calling him but thought if he'd really been interested in seeing her again, he would have gotten her number instead of putting the ball completely in her court.

The miles between her home and the clinic flashed by in a blur of colors and sounds. Her heart felt like it would beat out of her chest. She pulled up at the clinic, palms sweating. At least after today, she would have an answer.

4

Grant stretched out of the dark SUV, trying to rehearse the speech he was giving at Prescott University. He had a funny introduction, three main points why he should be senator, and an emotional closing. He focused on delivering the introduction with confidence and ease. Even after months on the campaign trail, speeches didn't come easy for him.

His phone buzzed, an unfamiliar number flashing across the screen. He declined the call, thinking it was probably more reporters or other politicians trying to raise money. It was ironic, even while running for the Senate, he'd been contacted by his opponent's camp trying to raise money. The young student who'd gotten an earful of why he would not support the esteemed Senator Walter Henry wouldn't make that mistake twice.

Grant brushed imaginary lint off of his charcoal gray suit. He glanced in the mirror one more time, then exited the SUV. A group of reporters rushed to intercept him.

A young, wiry guy with horn rim glasses and skinny jeans whose name tag read Mike Thomas stuck a microphone in Grant's face. "Mr. Harrington, do you think you have what it takes to beat four term senator like Senator Henry? He's been in the Senate almost as long as you've been alive!" The other reporters chuckled.

"If I didn't think I had any chance of winning, I wouldn't run." Grant paused, giving a smooth smile. "It's time we have a new face representing Mississippi in Washington. I think our state can be a leader in industry." *Remember the talking points. Stay on track. Industry, growth, education, healthcare.*

Mike frowned. "You've hardly any experience in local politics and no experience in national politics. Why do you think you could do a better job than Senator Henry?"

"Well, I served as mayor of State College for four years. And no, I don't have any experience working in federal government, but that's not always a bad thing. I'm not jaded. I'm excited to do this job, to help change Mississippi for the better. I'm in tune with our state, and I want to see the people here succeed. Not to mention, I served in our military, and I want to champion veterans to have the best healthcare money can buy." Grant straightened his tie and tried to ignore the perspiration forming on his forehead. *Better get used to these reporters and their questions.*

Mike smiled coldly at Grant. "Are you saying Senator Henry doesn't want the people of Mississippi to succeed?" *He's baiting me.* Grant took a deep breath and weighed his thoughts quickly. Any false move would find his words plastered all over the front page news.

"That's not what I said. I'm saying I bring a new perspective to our state. A younger, more in tune with the current circumstances perspective. Now, if you'll excuse me I have a speech to give. Hopefully, it'll answer many of your questions." He turned and started to walk up the steps.

Mike followed Grant. "Mr. Harrington, one more question before you go. Tell us a little about your family." This is the question he dreaded the most. Far worse than any question about policy.

"My father is my best friend. He raised me and provided a loving home and taught me all I know about being a good man. I'm thankful for him." Grant turned to leave but the same young reporter who tried to trap him before cornered him, sticking the microphone in his face.

"But what about your mother? You didn't mention anything about her." Maybe it was his imagination, but Grant thought he saw something in the Mike's eyes. Something that looked like joyful satisfaction. As if he already knew this was a sore spot for the aspiring senator.

"My mother and father are no longer married. No more questions, please." He bounded up the steps, forcing the reporters to move or be trampled.

He found the small dressing room and took a few moments to compose himself. When he approached the podium, he quickly glanced around the room, looking for her. It was an innate habit, one he was trying to train himself to stop. His mother left when he was nine and had not been back since.

Ever since she left, he'd catch himself looking for her in crowds, like somehow she would hear about something he was doing and come back to catch a glimpse of him. The worst time had been a musical in sixth grade, where he had left the stage in the middle of the show because he was sure he'd seen her in the back of the room. The poor woman didn't know what to do when a stranger embraced her in a tearful bear hug. It wasn't until he calmed down enough to really look that he realized it wasn't his mother. It was the single most mortifying and heartbreaking moment of his life.

Maybe that had been it. Somewhere along the line, he'd let the dream of his mother returning die. He still fought the urge to scan crowds, looking for her face. He often told himself it'd been thirty-three years since she left. He probably wouldn't recognize her now, even if she was right in front of his face. His dad offered to send him to counseling more than once over the years. Each time, Grant explained he was fine and didn't need it. After his high school sweetheart broke up with him, he'd gone for several sessions. Building a wall around his heart was much easier. Counseling peeled away the layers of hurt on a soul. Grant wanted no part of that then or now. It was much simpler to not need someone, so even if they left, it didn't hurt.

Grant delivered his speech as professionally and confidently as he could. He talked about how he wanted to reform education in Mississippi and fight more to help impoverished youth. He spoke about bringing industry to the rural Mississippi Delta and people find work. All in all, he felt like it had been a successful event. He'd answered a few questions from the reporters at the end, then retreated as fast as he could to the waiting SUV.

He checked his phone for the first time since he stepped out of the SUV several hours ago. He had two more calls from the same number that he did not recognize from earlier. *Probably some reporter.* He stuffed the phone back into his suit pocket.

For the first week or two after meeting Lila, he jumped to answer every number he didn't recognize, hoping it would be her. Every time, he'd been disappointed. After all this time, he decided she must not want to see him again. He could kick himself for not getting her number. The morning after their night together, he'd completely forgotten about an interview with a local newscaster, until his calendar alarm on his phone notified him. He rushed from her room down to his to brush his teeth and grab a clean shirt. He hadn't even had time to shower.

I probably looked like an ass leaving so quickly.

The SUV pulled up at Grant's small brick home off Robinson Avenue in downtown State College. He loved his little home. It was the perfect bachelor pad with its two bedrooms, two bathrooms, and a large living area for guests. He checked the mail, then punched in his father's number on his phone.

"Hello."

"Hey, Dad. It's me. Sorry I didn't get to talk much after the speech." Grant pulled a cold beer out from the fridge, taking a long, slow swig.

"You did great. Thought you hit the nail on the head several times as to what needs to be improved here, but you didn't get negative about your opponent. Well done."

"Thanks." He started to say something when that same number that called earlier popped up on call waiting. "This same number has been calling all day. Let me see what this is about." He clicked over to the other line. "Grant Harrington."

It was quiet in the small house, with only the refrigerator humming in the background. The beer bottle shattered the silence, as it slipped from Grant's hand.

5

Grant adjusted the seat belt, trying to get comfortable. He cancelled all his meetings and caught the first plane to D.C. Unfortunately, that meant a two hour layover in Atlanta, but he was on the way now. His mind raced as he thought about Lila. *I used a condom.* He'd had a few drinks that night, but nothing he couldn't handle. He sure as hell remembered to use a condom.

Why hadn't she called before now? Did she not feel a connection that night? His mind flashed back to their conversations at the Wisteria, her smiling up at him, dancing with him, pushing him against then wall in the stairwell. *Had she not felt that spark?* No, he knew she felt something, too. Lust, yes, but there was something more. Doubt filled his mind again. *I don't know her. Maybe she didn't feel anything. Maybe I was just some guy. Maybe that's why she didn't call.* He glanced out the window, watching fluffy clouds go by. *But I didn't get her number either.* He scrubbed his face with his hands. He knew he had to go see her, in person. Sort this mess out face to face. Maybe then he would know where they stood and how she really felt. *Maybe she would be willing to start over, see where this would go. There could be something special here. And is she's having my child, she's got to give us a chance.*

~

Lila tried to peel herself from the bathroom floor. She'd vomited three times that morning and couldn't imagine having anything left in her stomach. A sharp knock on the door startled her. Brushing her teeth quickly, she fought the nausea that bit at the back of her throat.

She walked to the door, as someone knocked again. She looked out the peephole, then turned away quickly, leaning back against the wall. Grant said he would come, but she didn't believe it until she saw him standing on her stoop. She ran a hand over her hair and pulled her robe even tighter. It was almost surreal to see him again, this man who'd completely changed her life.

Struggling to compose herself, she cracked the door open slightly, surprised that tears threatened to fill her eyes at the sight of him.

"Lila?" Grant's chocolate brown eyes stared at her, searching. "I'm so glad to see you." He leaned over and kissed her softly on the cheek. The gentle kiss surprised her. *I can't believe he came.* She rehearsed what she was going to say to him over and over, trying to decide on the right words before making that phone call. It made it worse that it took him forever to answer. She took a deep breath and tried to remember her manners.

"Come in." She gestured for him to have a seat on the sofa. "Do you want anything to eat? Maybe a drink?"

"No, I'm fine. I came here to see you, not eat."

Lila laughed nervously. "How was your trip?"

"It was good. Pretty uneventful." He ran his hand through

his dark hair. Silver glinted at his temples, and a memory flashed in Lila's mind. She remembered running her hands through that thick hair, tugging on it. She cleared her throat, pushing the memory back.

"Good. I'm glad you had an easy trip." She tried to think of what to say, anything to keep from having to talk about the elephant in the room.

"Have you been feeling any symptoms?" *Way to cut to the chase.*

"Had some nausea the past few mornings, but it usually gets better after morning time," she lied. For the past three days, she'd been nauseated until lunch and vomited one night after dinner. Grant's eyes roamed over her face. She didn't think she would be one of those glowing pregnant women.

"I'm sorry you've been sick. I can't believe this happened, Lila. I've never done anything like this before. I'm sure people say that, but I'm serious. I've only had one serious relationship, which was in college. I'm not the type of man who sleeps around. And I'm not the type of man who gets random women pregnant." *So that's what I am. A random woman.*

Her face must have betrayed her feelings. Grant blushed. "I don't mean you're a random woman. It's just you're not my girlfriend. I've never been so attracted to someone I would have sex with them on the first night." He raked a hand through that thick, salt and pepper hair. "We used a condom, for Christ's sake."

"I know." She shrugged. "Apparently, according to my doctor's nurse and the lovely Center for Disease Control website, even with perfect use, there's still an eighteen percent failure rate with condoms." She rolled her eyes. "Eighteen percent. That's eighteen unplanned pregnancies out of a hundred every year."

She walked over to the kitchen and poured a small glass of Sprite. "Do you want anything to drink?"

He looked pale. "No, thanks."

Lila paced in front of him before stopping to look at him head on. He was insanely handsome. "Look, Grant, we're both adults. We both made a decision and we'll both deal with the consequences. You don't have to try to make this something it wasn't."

"Well I don't regret it, even now. I don't regret it."

She was surprised by his words. She took a deep breath. "So, what do you want to do?"

"What do you mean what do I want to do? We're having a baby."

Thank you, genius. "Look, I'm thirty years old. I've never been married and have always wanted a family. I'm going to keep this baby and be the best mother I can be. I don't want you to feel obligated to be in the baby's life."

Irritation flashed across his face. "I want to be involved in our child's life. I need to be involved. It's my child, too." He paused. She thought he looked like he was struggling to get the words out. "There's something you need to know. I'm trying to win the Senate seat in Mississippi."

Just when she thought this man had already given her the biggest surprise of her life by getting her knocked up, he delivered another blow. "Senate? You want to be a senator? Jesus, Grant." She rolled her eyes. "Do you have any idea..." Her voice trailed off. *No, he didn't have any idea.* He didn't know who she was. Didn't know her last name. Didn't know what the hell he was getting into.

He paced back and forth across the living room. He raked his hands nervously through his hair. She finally got up, placed her hand on his arm and guided him back over to the sofa. "Sit down. You are making me nervous," she said. "We are going to be fine. We just need a plan."

"Well, I can't move here, not while the campaign is going on. How about you move to Mississippi to be close to me?"

"I don't know, Grant. My job's here. My family and friends… they're all here. My house for goodness's sake. Where would I live in Mississippi? What would I do?" She put her hands on her hips. "Why don't you stay in D.C. part of the time and Mississippi part of the time? That's what you would do if you won, anyways."

"Yes, but what would the media say? What reason would I have for being here all the time before I won the seat?"

She rolled her eyes. "You would have me. And our baby. Are those not good enough reasons?"

He pursed his lips. Frowning, he seemed to weigh his words. "I don't think you are thinking about the big picture here. As much as I hate it, my public image is at stake. This is just the kind of scandal my opponent would love to use against me."

Lila's face burned. "Scandal?" That's what I am to you?" She glared at him. "Well, maybe you should have thought more about your public image before sleeping with a random woman in a random inn."

He touched her leg. "I didn't mean that the way it sounded earlier." He sighed. "Look, if it wasn't for this Senate deal, I'd move here. We'd take it a day at a time and figure this out as we went. Unfortunately, it is what it is, and I need to come up with a way to make this work for us personally and work for me professionally."

"I'm all ears. You just let me know what you come up with." She got up, heading to the kitchen to pour another glass of Sprite.

Grant followed her into the kitchen, sitting down on the bar stool. He wrung his hands nervously, then looked her dead in the eye. "Let's get married."

"Married? Married! Have you lost your mind? Two days

ago, we didn't even know each other's last names and now you want to get married?"

Grant laughed at her. Her face burned. She fanned it, trying to cool down.

"Calm down. Let me finish what I was going to say. We can tell the press whatever you want. You were my secret fiancé, girlfriend, whatever. As early pregnant as you are, we may actually get away with the dates."

"And what if I don't want to be your political pawn?"

"I don't want you to be a pawn. I want you to be my wife, my partner in crime." He looked thoughtful. "I'll make it worth your while."

She felt like she could hardly breathe. *Married? As in for husband, wife, death do you part, married?* "You have lost your mind."

"Just hear me out. I've saved a lot of money up, from the time I was in college. Got a lot of scholarships, thank God." He sighed. "And if I win the Senate seat, I will have a pretty decent income from that and will continue to earn money off my accounting business."

"Are you really going to try to buy me?" *Maybe I don't know him at all. Why would I think I did? It was one night. I should know by now not to trust my heart.*

"I'm not trying to buy you, Lila. Don't insult me." His eyes looked dark, sharp. "I'm just trying to make this beneficial to you, since you would be doing this for me and my campaign. If I win you agree to stay married to me...say for, at least three years, I will pay you $100,000 for every year we are together. If I'm not elected, we stay married for six months after the election, just to make sure it looks legitimate."

Her mouth dropped open. "Then what?"

"I don't know." He threw his hands in the air, as if searching for an answer. "I'll give you $50,000 for all your trouble, and we'll quietly divorce."

"And what happens to me and the baby when this is all done? Will you still be involved?"

Grant looked insulted. "I'll pay child support and all educational expenses through college."

"So, you'll pay for the baby but will you actually be involved? You know, be a dad." *That's what's important. Not your money.* Grant's faced flushed. She knew she was walking a thin line. He looked ready to pounce. *I might pounce back.*

"Of course, I'll be his dad. I could never leave my child." He pulled at the collar of his shirt. "We'll need a confidentiality clause in the contract. Just to make sure it stays quiet."

"You don't trust me?" *Why would he? Why did I think I might be something special to him?*

Grant squeezed shoulder. "Yes, I trust you. But if we are going to make this a legal agreement, then I will need an attorney to draw up the papers for it. To protect both of us. It's just smart business. The attorney would be legally held to secrecy, too."

"I guess that makes sense." Lila twisted her hair. *Three years. If he won. If not, six months. Just long enough to fall in love and be left in the dust.*

"Think about it, ok? I'm going to go get a hotel. I'll give you some time, and we'll meet tomorrow. Will that work for you?"

She didn't say a word, only nodded. As he quietly shut the door, a single sparkling tear slid down her pale cheek.

6

Lila tossed and turned all night, mulling over Grant's proposal. All her life, she'd imagined finding someone to spend the rest of her life with, someone who would love her for who she really was, not as some trophy. There was no doubt in her mind her parent's marriage was, for all practical purposes, a marriage of convenience. She'd sworn she would never do the same.

Her mother would reminiscence about how she'd always known she wasn't cut out to marry "a common man." She'd grown up with a father who was a wealthy business man and had no intention of ever "living average," as she was fond of saying. Senator Ulysses Hudson was anything but average. He'd been in the Senate so long he was practically a national institution. Unbeknownst to anyone but his closest advisors and family, he was testing the waters to consider a run at the presidency in the next election.

Lila ran to the toilet, heaving up the remnants of her supper. While she thought it was rather early for morning sickness, apparently her baby wasn't following any specific timeline. *Her baby.* The words gave her a strange sensation in her chest. Fear and panic mixed with a strong sense of possession. She was going to have this baby and do the best she could to raise it in a loving, happy home.

She stood up shakily, wiping the back of her mouth on the hand towel before throwing it in the laundry hamper. She made her way to the kitchen. The clock on the microwave read 4:35 AM. *Way too early.* She poured herself a large glass of cold Sprite, forcing herself to sip it slowly. *Don't gulp.* That hadn't played out well last time. She nibbled on a few crackers before feeling like maybe her stomach had calmed down enough that she could think.

Her mind flashed to Kent. From what she'd learned since the disastrous wedding, Kent had been there all day. He'd gone through the motions of getting dressed in his tuxedo, even taking pictures with his family and groomsmen. They'd agreed to wait to take pictures together until after the cere-mony, in keeping with tradition of not seeing each other before the wedding.

She'd realized her mistake when she'd locked eyes with him at the end of the aisle. Even looking through the veil, she'd recognized his panic. He'd glanced around quickly, wiping his forehead. As she approached to the point where she had been instructed to stop and join hands with him, he shook his head several times. The words echoed in her head even now.

"Senator, I'm sorry. I'm so sorry. I just can't." He didn't even make eye contact with her. Without another word, Kent turned on his heel and ran out the side entrance of the cathe-dral, retreating somewhere into the back of the church.

She'd stood there stunned. Just stood there. Even her father, the ever verbose senator, didn't know what to do or say for a few moments. Thankfully, the kind minister placed his hand on her arm. "Dear, why don't you and your father leave out the side entrance, and I will handle the crowd." His soft voice somehow broke through to her stunned brain, bringing on full fledge panic.

She'd been too shocked to cry. Her best friend, Sophie Caine, found her first. Wordlessly, she'd hugged her. Sophie all but ripped the wedding dress off of her, then they fled. Together, they'd rode in silence to Lila's home. It wasn't until they reached her townhouse that emotions started hitting her. Pure rage and embarrassment. She still had the honeymoon airplane tickets in her purse. Sophie offered to go with her, but Lila knew it was a trip needed to make on her own.

The nausea welled up again, shocking her back to the here and now. She barely made it to the small half bath in the sitting room before falling to her knees beside the toilet. After washing her face, she laid down on the couch with her favorite blanket, finding *I Love Lucy* reruns on Hallmark. She tried to calm her mind, but it was useless.

Her whole life had been one big tug of war between pleasing her family and pleasing herself. She was Senator Hudson's daughter. Her face had been plastered all over the D.C. papers and gossip websites. During the "honeymoon," she'd made the mistake of searching for her name. There were at least 15 articles detailing the mortifying incident.

The day before she'd arrived at the Wisteria Inn, her phone had alerted her about an email from Kent. In a very succinct email, he explained he'd always admired her father and longed to be part of the Hudson legacy. While he said he thought he loved her, he'd realized after a conversation with her the night before the wedding, what he really loved was her last name and all that came with it. Lila told him the night before the wedding how she was so glad they were marrying for true love, not political gain. Kent said he realized if he married her, then he would be in fact, giving her what she feared most—a marriage not based on love. He wished her well and apologized for the horrible timing and embarrassment it might have caused her. She couldn't bring herself to respond.

As she tossed and turned on the couch, she thought of Grant. How ironic he was offering her everything she'd always wanted to avoid. At least, he was doing it upfront and not deceiving her the way Kent had. In a weird way, they would be full partners. Two people who knew their marriage wasn't built on love but on an agreement that could save face for both parties. Maybe she could even spin the situation with Kent? She didn't want to be the poor little rich girl who was left at the altar and then got knocked up by some random guy. Grant didn't want to be a single senator who had to hide his secret baby. This plan could save them both.

She could sacrifice three years, if he won. Three years to save her family's perfect image. Three years to save her reputation. Three years to give her child the basis of a normal childhood with two parents. She'd seen how fiercely Grant had spoken about being there for his child. She suspected no matter what she decided, he meant what he said. He would be a part of their child's life.

She stewed over what she knew would be required of a senator's wife. Public appearances, photo ops, luncheons, and speeches…all things she abhorred, but she could do it. She'd done it her whole life.

I will have to quit my job. She realized that didn't upset her in the least. *I'd have to live in Mississippi.* If she hadn't just driven through most of the state, this might have concerned her, but she loved Mississippi. Parts of the state had rolling hills and trees, which she found peaceful. The flat Delta land offered a unique way of life, with its blues bars and tamale trucks. And the coast…well, she'd fallen in love with the Mississippi coast. Not the water, as unfortunately, the murky Gulf waters were perpetually some shade of brown, but the coast's way of life. A little slower, a little snazzier, a little more artistic than other parts of the state. *I won't miss the D.C. traffic.* A lump formed in her throat. *But I sure will miss Sophie.* She glanced around her. *And my house.* She would keep the townhouse, though. She'd sublease it while she was gone.

All her life she'd sworn her marriage would be different than her parent's. She wanted to be in love with her husband and be loved in return for who she was. If she took this deal, she would be following her mother's footsteps by being used for what she could bring to the table politically. A cold, love-less marriage but respect and envy of others. She was ashamed she was considering going along with it.

*It could be different. He could love me. It might take time, but we had something that night. I know we did. Maybe with time, friendship and respect could lead to more...*She shook her head. *No. He made it clear this wasn't about me or the baby. It was all about him and his life. His campaign. His future. I don't matter to him. Not like that. He made that perfectly clear by presenting this deal. All business. No emotion. He doesn't want me. What happened that night was a fluke.*

After a while, she finally started to doze off. She awoke to hear a knock on the door. At least she'd gotten a few more hours of sleep. She peaked out the door to see Grant standing there with two cups of coffee in his hands.

She pushed her matted hair down, knowing she looked a fright. She pulled open the door, reaching instinctively for the coffee. Grant laughed, handing it over.

"I wasn't sure if it was ok with the baby or not."

"The doctor said a little caffeine isn't going to do any harm," she said, as she guzzled the coffee like a woman dying of thirst.

"Easy, easy. It's not going anywhere." Grant gently pulled the cup from her lips. "You'll make yourself sick."

"Oh, you missed that already. I'm actually feeling a little

better now." Grant's face paled. His look of concern warmed her heart. At least he wasn't completely insensitive.

"I don't want you to go through this alone. You didn't get in this situation alone, and I want to be there. Every day." *He sounds like he actually means that.* "Have you thought anymore about my offer?" *And there it is.*

Lila sat the coffee down and guided him to sit on the couch. Pulling her blanket around her, she fought the chill that ran down her spine. "Yes, I have. I've been up on and off all night thinking about it. I'll agree if we add one thing to the contract."

Grant frowned. "You name it."

I've got to protect my heart. She took a deep breath. "It has to explicitly say our marriage is in name only, and we both must remain faithful throughout the three years. I won't be subjected to that type of embarrassment."

"Name only?" Grant considered. "So, what happened at the Wisteria…?"

"Was uncharacteristic of me and won't be repeated. I only sleep with men I love, and I, well, I was in a very vulnerable emotional place when I met you." Grant didn't say anything for a while. She could tell he was weighing his options.

"Ok, we'll add it in to. Name only. No sneaking around with anyone else. Consider it done."

"Thank you, Grant." She tried to push down all the warning bells in her spirit telling her this was wrong. *This will save face for me and my family. Plus, I don't want to do this alone.*

He reached into his pocket and pulled out a small black box. He handed it to her. "This is for you." She opened the box to reveal an oval cut diamond with small baguettes on the side winked back at her. It had to have been at least 2 carats in the center stone. Maybe more. *It's perfect.*

Grant stared at her, gauging her reaction. "Do you like

it?" He looked nervous. As if her opinion on the ring actually mattered. She swallowed, then handed the box to him and offered her hand.

"It's stunning. Absolutely stunning." Her hand shook as he slipped the ring in place. Somehow, he'd gotten the size just right.

"I'm so glad you like it. I thought it was elegant." He smiled. "Just like you."

She looked at her hand, the diamond sending rays of fire dancing across the walls. The beauty of the ring only magnified the sense of loss in her heart.

7

I can't believe she said yes. Grant stared at his reflection in the mirror, still not believing this was real. A few days ago, he was simply trying to better his life and the life of those in his state by seeking a higher political office. Now, he was a man who'd made a deal to marry a woman he hardly knew. A woman who was carrying his child.

He hadn't been able to stop thinking about her since that night at the Wisteria. He'd thoroughly enjoyed their night together, but it was more than that. He'd felt a spark, something bubbling under the surface. Maybe it was the way she came flouncing into the bar, like she was looking to pick a fight. She'd about done it, too, when he'd laughed at her drink order.

He'd hoped she would have called after that night. *I guess if she hadn't gotten pregnant, I never would have heard from her.* He fantasized that maybe they could work this out, maybe start something new, but she squelched that idea before it even got going. She'd made it clear she had no desire to repeat their night at the Wisteria ever again.

Grant dressed, then called for a ride to Lila's house. He

had one more day in D.C. before he would fly back to Mississippi. They needed to make plans. He'd called his attorney the night. After calling in a few favors and sending some extra money, he was ensured the contract would arrive that afternoon.

I can't believe I'm actually have a contract made up for my marriage. Grant took a deep breath, trying to calm his nerves. He was stretched thin with the campaign. Stress had a whole new meaning now. Grant pulled out his phone, punching in his dad's number. After a few rings, Lawrence Harrington picked up the phone.

"Hello?"

"Hey, Dad. Sorry to call you so early. Just wanted to talk, if you aren't busy."

"Sure, what's on your mind? Is it the campaign?"

"That's part of it. I know we usually don't talk about Mom." He paused. "What do you think really happened with y'all?"

Lawrence was silent for several moments. "I don't know, Grant. I think part of it was she was disappointed in me. She married the idea of me, not the real me. When all the business fell apart, she didn't have any reason to be here."

"No reason to be here? She had us!" Grant fought the familiar anger that welled up in his chest. *Even if she didn't want you, how could she leave me?*

Lawrence cleared his throat. "I know. I loved your mother and would have done anything to make her happy. But we did alright, didn't we?"

Grant swallowed the hard lump in his throat. "Of course we did, Dad. You're the best." And he meant it. Lawrence Harrington was the type of dad most kids dreamed of having. Attentive, fun, dependable. "I just don't understand. I mean, I hate to say it, Dad, but I understand leaving a husband. Things happen between a man and a woman we can't always explain or justify. But a child? How can a mother leave her child? I just don't think I'll ever understand that."

"It was her loss, Grant. How she could leave you, I will never know. You have been the biggest blessing in my life."

Grant sighed. Questions that will never have any real answers. "I know there's no simple answer. Just had it on my mind. Do you, well…do you think I have what it takes to be a good husband? "

"Husband?" Lawrence chuckled. "You got some secret girlfriend I don't know about?"

Oh boy, do I. Grant shook his head slightly. "Well, actually, yes. There's someone special. She lives in D.C., so that's why you haven't met her. It's been a whirlwind, and I didn't want to say anything yet."

Dead air filled the line for a moment. Grant cleared his throat. "Dad, you there?"

"Um, yes, just trying to process how my son could have a woman so special he's thinking of marriage and not tell me about her before now?"

"It's a long story. I'll tell you more when we talk face to face. I'm actually in D.C. now to see her. I better get off of here, but just wanted to call."

"Well, this isn't the last of this conversation. But to answer your question, I think you will make someone a fine husband."

Grant breathed a sigh of relief. He didn't know what it was, but he felt better hearing his father say it, even if the marriage was a sham. "Thanks, Dad. Talk to you soon."

He hung up the phone and ran a hand over his eyes. He didn't know why after all these years, it still stung about his mother. He tried to make peace with it, but the wound would always be there.

Grant shook his head trying to clear the thoughts of his mother away. He grabbed his bag and jacket, then headed out to meet the car. He rode through the winding streets of D.C. before arriving at Lila's red brick townhouse in Georgetown. She opened the door and actually looked happy to see him. She smiled, causing a dimple to pop out in her left cheek, then pushed her blond hair back from her shoulders.

The sparkling diamond on her left hand glinted in the sun. He still couldn't believe she was going be his wife.

"Come in," she said, while ushering him in. He sat on the plush sofa, looking around the room. She sat down in a pale blue wingback chair, crossing her slim legs in front of her. "I've been thinking. With your senate campaign, we really need to try to avoid the impression of a shotgun wedding."

Smart girl. "I agree. We need to come up with something that will sound good to the media."

"Exactly. I've been thinking we could say we met in the Bahamas in February and had a whirlwind romance. That way it ties into everything in the press about me."

Grant frowned. "What are you talking about?"

Lila's faced turned bright red. "You haven't searched me on the internet? Come on, Grant. I would have thought you would have done a little more research on your future wife."

"Ummm…no, I haven't." Panic filled his chest. Maybe he should have done more checking.

"Well, I'm not a murderer or anything like that. Calm down." She giggled, placing her hand on his shoulder. "Just a jilted rich girl."

"I don't think I understand."

"Senator Ulysses Hudson. Ring a bell?" Of course, Grant knew who Senator Hudson was. He was on the national news every other day for one thing or another and a star in the Democratic Party.

"Yes, I know who Senator Hud…" Grant felt all the blood drain from his face. "Wait, Hudson. Lila Hudson. You're Senator Hudson's daughter?"

A bashful smile crossed Lila's face. She seemed to enjoy the fact that he didn't realize she was political royalty. On top of that, she was political royalty for the other team. Grant was a staunch Republican.

"The one and only. So, when my fiancée left me at the altar in front of a few hundred folks, it caused quite a sensation."

"Fiancée? You were engaged? He felt dizzy. "Are you still involved with him?"

"No, no, not at all." She rolled her eyes, as if it was a ridiculous thought.

Grant took a deep breath. "So, the trip to the Bahamas?"

"My honeymoon for one." He saw a glint of tears in her eyes. She wiped her eyes quickly. "I'm not crying over him. I'm not. It was just so humiliating. Stupid hormones." She grabbed a tissue from the end table by the sofa and dabbed at her eyes.

"I had no idea. I'm so sorry, Lila. Did he say why?"

"Well, he sent me a short email, basically saying he only wanted my father's approval and to be Senator Hudson's son in law. At least he didn't go through with it. I just wish he'd dumped me in private. Not left me standing at the altar looking like a dumb ass." She struggled to control her emotions. "So, thanks to that lovely debacle, we have to come up with a pretty tight timeline."

He let the information sink in. *I'm going to look like a rebound. Or worse, someone who's taking advantage of her.* "This definitely changes things. We're going to have to be very precise about our timeline. So, we meet in the Bahamas. I'm your shoulder to cry on. We have a hot and heavy love affair. I propose."

"Yes, and I think we really put it out there. Sell it to the press. Lots of public appearances, lots of hand holding, kissing, etc. Show them we mean it."

"And if they see through it?"

"How can they prove anything? The attorney is sworn to secrecy, and we are the only two who know. Plus, when we have a baby in a few months, then they will know the marriage is legit."

"Do you want to get married here?" Grant asked.

"Hell, no." She rolled her eyes. "I can't go through that media circus again. We could call Wisteria Inn. It's such a small venue, we could keep it an intimate ceremony. Just a few friends and family, then we could release the photos to the press. I've still got a wedding dress. Sophie, my best friend, can be my maid of honor and just wear her brides-maid dress from the wedding."

Grant nodded. "That would work. I'll call them. We've only got one weekend left in March."

She checked the calendar on her phone, then chuckled. "Ummm...Let's see. I think we should do it as soon as possi-ble, but we'll have to make a few plans. Maybe April fifth?" She got up and walked into the kitchen, then poured a glass of Sprite. "Want some?"

He shook his head no and didn't even bother checking his schedule. If there was something planned, he would move it. "The fifth works." He followed her into the kitchen, then did a quick internet search on his phone for the Wisteria's number. A few minutes later, it was all confirmed.

"Done. We'll have it in the garden, weather permitting. If it's raining, they have a small ballroom we can use. I also booked Noelle's for the reception."

"Well, that was easy enough." She stared down at the floor.

"Are you ok?" He wanted to reach out and hold her. Kiss her. Comfort her.

She shrugged. "I'm fine. Just never thought I would be left

by a man who I thought loved me and marry a man I hardly know."

"Well, we need to work on that. Knowing each other." He reached over to touch her cheek. "I'm a nice guy. A good dancer if you remember correctly. We had a lot in common."

She clutched at her thin silver necklace. "Yes...yes, I guess you are right." *She doesn't want this to go anywhere. I don't even know why I should try.*

"I guess I better get going. Got to catch my flight back. We'll talk more this week." She walked him to the door. Before he left, he kissed her softly on the mouth. Little flames of desire ignited in his chest. He didn't know how well it was going to work being so attracted to a woman he was supposed to keep his hands off of. Especially since that woman was carrying his child. He pulled back and looked into her blue eyes.

Her full lips parted, and her skin flushed. She swallowed. "Talk to you soon." She fumbled with the lock, then opened the door. He walked to the car, glancing over his shoulder. She'd already shut the door. *Maybe it would be easier if I lost the campaign. Then we could fade into obscurity, get divorced, and move on with our lives. Maybe I could find someone who would really love me.* He tried to ignore the nagging voice asking him if he could recover when Lila left him, whether he won or not.

∾

A pril 5, 2014

Lila watched as the hairdresser looped her blond hair around the curling iron. *Clip, twist, release.* The hair dresser teased and sprayed, gathering the curls back with a rhinestone and pearl clip. The week before, Lila decided she couldn't wear the same dress she'd worn when she walked down the aisle toward Kent. She just couldn't do it.

Her original dress was a Cinderella style ball gown. It weighed a ton and looked like something a princess would wear. Lila loved it, but the thought of putting it on again made her feel sick.

After spending some time trying to soothe Sophie's hurt feelings from not knowing anything about her mystery lover from the Bahamas, she'd talked Sophie in to shopping all over Georgetown looking for a wedding dress. Thankfully, she wasn't showing and had even lost some weight from all the morning sickness.

She had about given up hope of finding a dress that day, until they went into a small vintage boutique. Then, she found The One. She was told the dress was from the late 1950s. The snug bodice and long, lacy sleeves fit her like a glove. The A-line skirt fell perfectly at her feet. It didn't even need altering.

Her mother wanted to have brunch, but she just couldn't bring herself to do it. She was about to embark into the one thing she said she would never do, and she didn't need living proof of marrying for money and power eating pancakes with her that morning. Sophie made up a bunch of excuses to get Delores off of Lila's back so she could have some breathing room. Lila wanted to tell Sophie about the agreement but was sworn to secrecy. It was part of the contract.

It'd been hard enough lying her way through the phone call with her boss, trying to explain how she wouldn't be coming back to Georgetown University because she'd fallen in love with a man from Mississippi. She'd dropped off her written notice effective immediately and had packed up her office in an hour. She still couldn't believe she'd quit her job.

Lila handed the hair dresser a check, then it was just her and Sophie in the small dressing room now. Her mother was outside schmoozing the guests. Sophie finished applying her makeup, then turned to Lila. "So, how do I look?" Sophie twirled around so Lila could see her in all of her full bridesmaid glory. The recycled navy bridesmaid dress looked perfect with her mahogany hair. To mix it up a little, Sophie had the dress altered to make it tea length to be more fitting for a garden wedding, instead of wearing the full evening gown it had once been.

She's my best friend, and I can't even tell her. Everything is so messed up. Everything. Lila took a deep breath. She pulled Sophie in a tight hug. "You are going to steal the show looking so beautiful."

"Whatever." Sophie rolled her eyes. "I can't wait to meet this mystery man. I bet Grant's going to die when he sees you in that dress." Lila forced herself to smile. Pretend to be the joyous bride. She smiled harder.

"I hope so." She smoothed her hands over the skirt. "I know it sounds crazy to you, Soph. And I'm sorry you haven't met him yet."

Sophie clasped Lila's hand. "Look, I'm not trying to rain on your parade. I'm not. But I'm your best friend, so I gotta ask. You're sure this isn't a rebound thing?"

Play it cool. She's got to believe you. Lila squeezed her friend's hand. "No, it's not. I know the timing is weird." Sophie arched one perfect eyebrow. Lila stumbled on. "Ok, it's weird. It's crazy. You don't think I know that?" Lila sighed. "You of all people know I wasn't in the right state of mind to meet a man when I left here for the Bahamas. But it happened." She smiled. "And I'm glad it did. Kent was a mistake."

Sophie dropped her hand. "Kent was an ass. I still can't believe he did that to you. After all those years together..." She shook her head. "I just think you need to take some time. It wouldn't hurt to actually date for a while."

Lila averted her eyes away from her friend. *I hate lying to her.* She sighed. "I don't expect you to understand, okay? And you don't have to. I just need you to be my best friend. Just be here." She grabbed Sophie's hands, holding them tightly. "Just be my best friend."

Sophie stared at her for a moment. She cleared her throat. "Alright. I tried."

Lila knew if the tables were turned, she'd probably be screaming at the top of her lungs asking Sophie what in the world she thought she was doing. *She's a better person than me.*

Sophie fished around in her bag before pulling out a tiny lace handkerchief. "This was Granny's. We didn't do the something borrowed, something blue thing last time, and well…this time I'm not taking any chances." She handed the handkerchief to Lila.

The soft lace and cotton handkerchief was mono-grammed with baby blue initials. "Thanks, Soph. Something borrowed, old, and blue." Lila touched her ring. "This is my something new." The diamond winked back at her. "Plus, I guess the dress can be both old and new. Old but new to me. All the bases are covered."

She stepped into the dress, then eased her arms into the sleeves. "You gotta help me lace this thing up." Sophie pulled the laces on the back of the dress tight.

Lila turned to face the mirror. Sophie wrapped an arm around her shoulders. "This dress suits you. That ball gown was Senator Hudson's daughter's dress. This is you." That simple statement caused tears to spring into her eyes. Lila fanned her face, determined not to mess up her makeup.

"Stop that talk…Can't mess up all this work." She hugged Sophie, then grabbed her bouquet. "I think it's about show time."

As she got closer to the room just inside the doors that led to the garden, she saw her father. Senator Hudson made a dashing figure in his suit. She lifted her face up and brushed her lips across his cheek. "Hey, Dad."

He smiled, but the smile didn't reach his eyes. "Lila. You look beautiful, honey."

"Thank you." She leaned her ear against the door. *Let's get this over with.* "Only a few more minutes now."

For once in her life, she thought Ulysses Hudson looked nervous. "Dad, what is it?"

"This whole thing, Lila." He frowned. "Look, I know the thing with Kent was bad...I know. And I'm sorry he did that to you. None of us saw that coming." He clenched it jaw. "Believe me, if I had, I'd handled him long before it got to that point."

"Dad, it wasn't your fault. It wasn't." *I can't do this. Not now.* The music changed. One more song before the wedding march would start.

"Look, you don't have to do this. You hardly know this man. Your mother and I are very concerned and..."

Lila interrupted him. "Dad, I love him. I'm happy. Just walk me down the aisle, ok?" She slipped her arm through his, breathing deeply, slowly. Her mind was back to the last time she prepared to walk down the aisle. The time when she was abandoned and humiliated.

Grant wouldn't do that. She took a few more deep breaths. *I'm Senator Hudson's daughter. I can do this for my family and my baby.* She instinctively touched her abdomen. *I'm not going to embarrass myself or my family any more than I already have.* Steadying herself, she squared her shoulders and waited until she heard the first notes to the wedding march. She smiled at her father and stepped out of the door toward her future.

God, she's beautiful. As she walked toward him, her eyes stayed on his. Grant's heart skipped in his chest. *I can't believe we are doing this.* His mind flashed back to seeing her walk into the Wisteria Inn for the first time. He remembered their one night of passion together...the heat, the excitement. *She's really going to be my wife.*

As she approached him, he noticed the bouquet she held was shaking. *What am I doing to her? I don't' want her to be miserable. Maybe in time, she will love me. Or at least remember that at some point, she liked me.* When she finally stood before him, he reached for her hand. She grasped his hand tightly, but he could still feel the tiny tremors causing it to shake. He squeezed her hand softly.

"Hi," he whispered. She looked up at him, smiling shyly.

"Hi," she whispered back. The pastor started speaking, greeting the small audience. They'd stuck to their agreement to keep it a small wedding. Lila's family, who he had just met that morning, sat on the front row. Unbeknownst to Lila, Grant endured an hour long interrogation by Ulysses and

Delores and had to explain why he wanted to marry their daughter so quickly.

Grant's father stood to the right of him, while Sophia flanked Lila on the left. Nick, his campaign manager and best friend, was on the front row. His aunt, three cousins, and a few other friends rounded out his side of the congregation.

The pastor said a short sermon, then walked them through the vows. He heard himself saying, "I, Grant, take you, Lila, to be my lawfully wedded wife..." Before he knew it, he was reaching for the thin diamond band his father held, and slipping the ring onto the third finger of her left hand.

J ust like that and I'm married. It happened so fast. Lila went through the motions of cutting the cake. Sophie gave a short sweet speech, which got a genuine laugh out of Lila. The photographer constantly flashed his camera. She smiled until she felt like her face would cracked wide open. They lined up with her family, then his family, then their families together.

Somebody handed her a flute of champagne. She remembered clinking her glass against Grant's, smiling as if she been waiting for this her whole life. They cut the small round wedding cake. Grant shoved cake into her mouth getting a small bit on her nose. She laughed as she brushed it off, while the camera flashed in the background. *No one looking from the outside would realize the whole marriage was a sham.*

In what seemed like a matter of minutes, people were leaving, then she was climbing the same wooden staircase to the same room they'd spent their only night together.

I hope he doesn't think that's happening again. Because it's not. When they reached the door, Grant slid the key in, holding the door open for her. He flipped the sign to DO NOT DISTURB, waiting on her to walk into the room, almost as if they were about to walk back in time.

She looks scared to death. Grant placed his hand on Lila lower back. "Lila, it's okay. I'm going to hold up our agreement. No sex, remember?" She smiled weakly. *Don't cry. Please don't cry.*

"I know you will. It's not that. I just…well, I can't believe I'm married." She walked over and sat on the edge of the bed. "It's crazy to think how quickly it can happen. It's like, maybe five minutes, and it's done." Grant walked over and sat down on the edge of the bed, removing his jacket.

"I know." He snapped his fingers. "Just like that." He flashed back to the night they spent together in this very bed. "This baby changed everything for both of us. But I want you to know it's a good change. We're going to be okay." Her lip trembled and she wiped her hand over her eyes. *Don't cry.*

"I'm sorry," she said. "It's just overwhelming me, I think. Stupid hormones." She sat down beside him. He placed his hand on her shoulder, squeezing it gently. He pulled her into a big bear hug, running his hand up and down her back.

"Lila…" He leaned forward and pressed his lips softly to hers. She gasped, then hesitantly kissed him back slowly, softly at first then more urgently. She raked her fingers through his hair, then trailed her lips across his cheek. His hands raced across the thin material. The frail lace seemed so delicate, he knew he could rip it off with one swift tug. He felt down the back of her gown, reaching the tiny ribbons holding the dress on to her slim body. He untied the ribbons slowly.

She sighed, pulling back. "Grant, wait. We had a deal."

He froze. "I'm sorry." He held his hands up in surrender. "It's just…I don't know. Won't happen again."

She looked like she might say something more but shook her head. "It's fine. I just don't want things to get out of hand." She grinned. "I think that's how we got in this mess in the first place." *This mess.* It was a sharp reminder to him that this was a loveless marriage. A marriage to protect both of their reputations.

"Yes, of course. Well, I think I'm going to change then get some sleep." He tried to control his emotions.

She frowned, looking down at her dress. "I need you to help with my dress."

"I can do that." She stood up and turned around so he could work the ribbons again. He fumbled and even cursed a few times at the tiny hooks and ribbons. His fingers brushed against her smooth, warm skin. He fought to keep his thoughts off of throwing her back against the bed and making her change her mind about the stupid addendum to their contract.

When she was finally able to step out of the dress, he felt his blood stir. She held the dress tightly to her chest, covering her small breasts. She grabbed her bag and retreated to the bathroom. Grant changed out of his suit, pulling on a pair of thin blue pajama pants. He'd already crawled into bed when she returned out of the bathroom. She was wearing a soft pink gown that hit right above her knees. He could tell she was trying to be conservative and not tempt him, but he was tempted all the same. She turned off the light and crawled into bed next to him, careful not to touch him. They lay there in silence for several minutes before she turned on her side away from him. As he lay there in the darkness, Grant tried to comprehend what he had done. He worried that not only was he changing their lives forever, but there would be a new little person whose life would be affected by every decision they made.

10

Lila woke up with a start. She couldn't move. At some point during the night, Grant curled around her. *Where am I?* The day before came rushing back. She really was Mrs. Harrington.

As she stared down at Grant, a wave of nausea rose up and had her slinging his arm off of her. She ran to the bathroom, coughing, trying to fight the urge to vomit. She clutched the sink, trying to steady herself before quickly dropping to her knees by the toilet. Grant rushed into the bathroom, slamming the door against the wall when he opened it. His hair was sticking straight up, as he looked frantically around the room. *Like a bull in a china shop.* If she hadn't felt so bad, Lila would've laughed.

"Are you okay?" He leaned down placing his hand on her back, rubbing it in slow, rhythmic strokes.

"Not really, but it will pass." *Dear Lord, please don't let me vomit in front of him.* "Grant, it's okay. Go back to bed. I'll be fine. I just need to sit here for a few more minutes."

"I'm not leaving. You'll just have to get used to me being here." He smiled charmingly. She shoved her hand against his chest, gritting her teeth against the bile in her throat. "Get out. Get out, get out, get out."

Grant backed away. "Okay, okay. If you need anything, I'll be right outside the door."

"Thank you." He got up and shut the door softly. She clenched her jaw for about five more seconds, then vomited violently. She laid on the bathroom floor for about fifteen more minutes before deciding it was safe to go back to bed. She washed her face, then brushed her teeth.

Crawling back in the big warm bed, she tried not to make eye contact with her husband. He stared at her questioningly. She didn't respond. Without saying anything, Grant reached over and covered her up with the quilt. He curled himself around her and wrapped her up in his big arms. She wanted to protest, but he felt so good to her chilled body she finally gave in and snuggled closer.

She started to drift off to sleep with Grant reached over to set the alarm on his phone. "We've got an hour or so before we have to start getting dressed." He kissed her temple.

"Do you have something planned?" She looked over her shoulder, trying to meet his eye. Unsuccessful, she turned around to face him. She looked up in those dark eyes. *How does he look so good in the morning?* She touched a hand to her hair. *I'm sure I look like a grease monkey.* He gave her a peck on the nose.

"Well...." he grinned, then shrugged. "I wanted to surprise you. I thought we needed something that resembled a honeymoon. You know, so the marriage looks legitimate."

"A honeymoon? What about our deal?" *I'm not having sex with him again. Nope. Not doing it. He can flash that smile all day with those bedroom eyes. Not getting my heart broken.*

"Keep your panties on. It's just two days in Ocean

Springs, a little coastal town here on the Gulf. We can eat, relax. Walk down Main Street. You can shop."

She rolled her eyes. "If I remember correctly, my panties are what got us in this mess in the first place." She pursed her lips when he started laughing. "Shut up!" She couldn't help but laugh, too. She pulled the pillow over her head. "Just wake me up when I need to get ready."

~

Grant twirled the dial to the eighties channel on his radio. Michael Jackson belted out hit after hit as they drove in silence. Lila had her blond hair thrown up in a loose knot and big sunglasses hiding her eyes. She'd slept like the dead until he woke her up to get ready for the trip. He'd catch himself watching her, then look away when she caught him. He felt like he was in junior high again, ogling the cheerleader. Except the cheerleader was his wife.

"Were you a cheerleader in high school?"

Lila looked at him like he'd lost his mind. "What?"

"Cheerleader? Rah rah, go team? Short skirts?"

She glared at him. "I know what a cheerleader is, thank you very much. Where did that come from?"

"Just thinking it's like I married the hot cheerleader from high school." He winked and squeezed her leg.

Lila rolled her eyes but smiled. "Yeah, I admit it. I cheered. But only my sophomore and junior year. I was over it after that." She pulled her glasses down to look in the small mirror in the sun visor. "I'll take the compliment though." She raised an eyebrow. "What about you? You seem like an athlete."

Grant grimaced. "Eh, not so much. I was skinny, quiet, and liked to read and write. I'm sure you can let your imagination tell you my high school status." He remembered Shane Vasquez beating the snot out of him after school more than once, just because he could. "High school wasn't really the best for me, but college... well, college was fun."

He didn't mention how he'd grown four inches in between the senior year of high school and his freshman year of college. His dad encouraged him to lift weights, and next thing he knew, Grant was having girls chase him. He smiled at the memory.

Lila sized him up. "High school is hard for everyone. One way or the other. Everyone wanted to be my friend because of my father, but they really didn't want to be my friend. Just use me to go to cool parties and have Dad pay for stuff." She paused. "I met Sophie in college, thank God. She could care less who my father is."

"I never thought about it like that. Your dad being who he is, well, that makes you more of a target for all kind of stuff." He exited off the interstate onto the quaint Main Street in Ocean Springs. Rows and rows of shops sprung up in between large oak trees draped with Spanish moss. "See that store? It's an old-fashioned drug store. Has a real soda fountain where they make ice cream floats, and you can sit at the counter and drink bottled Cokes. Just like the 1950s." He loved that place. All of a sudden, he felt foolish. She'd probably traveled the world. Going to some small town in Mississippi wasn't going to impress her.

"Is that a toy store?" She squealed. "I love toy stores!" She turned to stare back at the store as they drove past. "I collect children's books."

"Well, now, see that's something I didn't know about you. You can read them to the baby." *The baby.* He still couldn't believe he was having a baby. An image of Lila reading to a little girl filled his head. For some reason, he thought it would be a girl but hadn't shared that with her.

Lila touched her belly. Her voice was soft when she replied, "Yes, yes, I can." He steered the SUV into the parking spot in front of a large, white antebellum home with a big wrap around porch and glider rockers on the porch.

"We're here." He left her in the car to run in and get the key. A few moments later, he'd unloaded their bags, and they were opening the door to the honeymoon suite. He'd gone with his gut instinct, hoping Lila would like his choice. She gasped slightly when he opened the door. Hopefully, that's a good sign. She started to step into the room, but he grabbed her arm.

"Come on now, it's tradition." He scooped her up and carried her over the threshold.

"Grant!" Lila wound her arms around his neck and giggled. He placed her gently on the edge of the small sofa, thinking that was a safer choice than the bed.

"So, what do you think?" She turned gazed around the room. It was a soft blush pink, with thick, fancy crown molding tracing the top and bottoms of the walls. A large, heavy antique mahogany bed was against one wall. Pink and cream satin linens draped the bed. A large gold gilded mirror hung across from the bed over a heavy marble topped dresser. They'd stepped back into the 1800s, and from the look on her face, Lila liked it.

"It's stunning. Absolutely stunning." She trailed a hand across the marble top on the dresser. "Look at this furniture. My grandmother had a piece like this. It had been passed down through the years."

"I'm so glad you like it. How about we get settled then go downtown?"

Her face lit up. "Sounds perfect."

An hour later, they'd changed clothes and unpacked. Lila came back out of the bathroom wearing a pale blue dress with silver sandals. He'd changed into khaki shorts and a dark green t-shirt, before throwing on his weathered brown Sperrys. He took her hand, as they walked to the front desk.

He spoke briefly to the receptionist, then headed for downtown.

"Oh, Grant, it's just beautiful." Lila squeezed his hand. "It reminds me of a smaller version of Charleston." Main Street was lined with oak trees, which acted as a canopy over the sidewalks. Spanish moss draped itself over the branches like a clingy lover. The air was warm, but not the muggy, stifling heat the South was known for. Not yet anyways. That would come in the next few months. Rows of small shops lined the streets. Some were stately brick, other whimsical colors of turquoise, magenta, or lavender. The colors blended together, painting a fun, vibrant backdrop.

"It really does remind me of Charleston, now that you mention it." He smiled at an elderly couple who passed them on the sidewalk. Lila squeezed closer to Grant to keep from running into them. He caught a whiff of her peach shampoo and smiled. Without thinking, he bent down to kiss her on the top of the head. She looked up surprised but smiled at him. *Maybe there is a chance we could have something. Maybe I haven't ruined everything between us after all.*

"Let's go in the toy store first." She pulled him in to the store, where vintage toys from childhoods gone by lined the shelves. There were some they recognized from their own childhoods, such as My Little Ponies, Lite Brites, Teenage Mutant Ninja Turtles, and Easy Bake Ovens. Candy Land, jacks, hula hoops, and Frisbees were stacked in various places.

Lila squealed with delight when she spotted rows and rows of books. Before Grant knew what was happening, she'd racked up over a hundred dollars in dolls, games, trucks, and books.

He toted her bags out as they strolled down to the next store. "Dolls and trucks?"

She raised an eyebrow. "Well, we don't know what we are

having. I could always save them for the next one." Her face turned red. "I mean…I don't know why…"

Grant squeezed her hand. "It's ok." He tried to not think about her words, but the thought reverberated in his head. *The next one.* If they kept up this agreement, there wouldn't be a next one. At least, not with each other. *Maybe over time, she'll give us a chance. Maybe this little one could have a brother or sister.*

She spotted the old-fashioned drug store. "You feel like some ice cream?"

Grant pushed back his thoughts of the future. *Focus on now.* "Sure. They have wonderful praline ice cream here." A few moments later, they were both eating scoops of ice cream out of waffle cones. Lila trailed a foot across the barstool down to the black and white checked floor.

"I love it here. For the first time in a long time, I'm relaxed." She pushed her blond hair back from her face. "I hope you're having a good time, too?"

"Wouldn't want to be anywhere else." He looked around. "No reporters, no campaigning. No Nick." He chuckled. "I love Nick. It's why I picked him to be my campaign manager. He's my best friend. When Mom…." He paused, surprising himself at the memory. "My parents divorced when I was young. Nick, let me spend the night at his house every weekend for the next two months. His mom became a mother to me. His family took me to movies, ballgames, the park. They even invited me and Dad to go to the beach with them every year."

"Sounds like Nick comes from good people." She traced a thumb across his hand.

He shook his head. "Thanks." He looked down, reminding himself there was nothing to be embarrassed about. He couldn't help what his mother did. "So yeah, Nick…he's my best friend. But we've spent a little too much time together lately. It's nice to get away."

They ended up going in to several other shops. Grant found an oil painting of the Biloxi lighthouse at the 4th of July, with red, white, and blue fireworks exploding against an onyx sky. He loved the painting, not only for Independence Day, but for his home state. *It'll make the perfect addition to my office, if I win.*

Lila admired a dainty mother of pearl and silver bracelet, so he bought it for her after she'd moved on to the next shop. They found a tiny bakery displaying perfect white petit fours with delicate pink roses. They purchased half a dozen before heading back to the room.

Lila flounced down on the bed, kicking off her shoes. "This really has been so much fun." Her blue eyes sparkled as she looked at him. He remembered that night at the Wisteria, talking in front of the fireplace with her. An idea hit him.

"I'm so glad you are enjoying it. I've got an idea for tonight, if you don't mind letting me do some errands without you."

She frowned. "Ok...I packed a new novel, so I'll rest and read for a while."

"Perfect." He mentally added up what he needed to do to get things set up. "I'll let you know when I'm headed back, so you can start getting ready." He hesitated, then bent over her and pressed his lips to hers. She inhaled sharply, surprised, before melting against him. He deepened the kiss, feeling his control weaken. He wanted her. He leaned into her, until he was pressed against her, sliding his leg between hers. She moaned, moving closer, pulling him toward her. He slid a hand up her dress, stroking her smooth thigh. His mind seemed to blur until all he could think about was the sharp need fisting hard in his gut. She moved back, just enough to break their contact. She placed a hand on his chest, pushing him further away.

"Grant," she whispered. "Please, we...we said we wouldn't." He forced himself to focus, feeling rejected, horny, irritated, and needy all at the same time. He moved away from her, sitting up on the side of the bed.

"I know...I'm sorry." He stood up, straightening his shirt. "I'll let you know when I'm headed back." Before she even had time to reply, he left the room, slamming the door behind him.

∽

G rant texted her with a heads up to start getting dressed. He'd told her it would still be another thirty minutes or so before he left his last stop, so she had plenty of time to get out of the shower before he got back. She'd tried to relax, nap, read, but all she could think about was that kiss. Why had she pushed him away? Why did they even have that stupid clause? They'd been together before. Sex was one thing that apparently came easy to them. Attraction was there. *Check.* That was not a problem. It was all the other things. Love, commitment, a real relationship. Those were the issues. Should she just give in? *At least enjoy some fun in this loveless marriage?*

Her mind raced, as she turned on the shower and stepped under the scalding water. *The whole reason I made him agree to no sex was to protect my heart. He doesn't love me. A baby and a few more rolls in the hay won't change that.* She lathered her hair with shampoo. *But what if it did? Could he love me? Would he open his heart to the possibility?*

As soon as the thought entered her mind, she pushed it away. *No, he wouldn't.* Sex and love were two very different things. Especially to a man. She would keep up her end of the bargain, even if he pushed the limits. No sex, and she would remain in control of her feelings and protect her heart.

She'd just finished blow drying her hair, when she heard the key slide into the lock. Grant flashed those perfect teeth, causing her heart to skip a beat. "Sorry it took me so long." He grabbed a few items from the closet.

"It's alright." She brushed her hair nervously. "I'm excited to see what this surprise is."

"I hope you like it." He grabbed his toiletry kit and headed to the bathroom. "It won't take me long, then we can get on the way."

Grant maneuvered the car in and out of traffic until he found the correct turn off spot. He parked, then opened the car door for Lila. She looked like someone out of a movie, with her yellow sundress and silver sandals. She'd brought a heavy white sweater at his insistence, even though it had been in the seventies all day. He'd worried it would get cool at night. He was pleased to see the bracelet he'd bought her wrapped around her wrist. "Ok, we're here." A few scraggly scrubs and a small tree blocked the view of the surprise. "It's just past here, so I want you to close your eyes until we get there."

"Ummmm, ok."

"I'm not an ax murderer, remember?"

"Yeah, I'm still banking on that being the truth." The sun was setting, splashing reds, pinks, and purples across the skyline.

"Just shut your eyes and hold my hand." She took his hand. He led her down a few steps and out onto the sand. Waves crashed against the white sand, making a perfect backdrop. "Ok, turn around. There's a chair behind you. Sit there with your eyes shut. No peeking."

She squeezed her eyes shut tightly, scrunching her face up at him sarcastically. She ran a hand over the chair, making sure she found the seat before gingerly lowering her body down. "Ok, now what?"

"Now, just hold on a minute." He made a few adjustments to the setup, putting supplies in the right places, and silently handed cash to the men he'd found to get everything in order. The men nodded at him silently and waved goodbye. *Who says money can't buy just about anything?*

"Ok, now look."

She opened her eyes, taking it all in. Surprise flashed across her face. She pointed to a large white screen. "What's that?"

"That's part of your surprise. Dinner and a movie on the beach." He'd hired the men, who he'd found working at a local videography company, to set up a projector, which ran off of a generator and large white screen. He'd bought a large white sheet, tons of fresh flowers, and candles, along with a picnic basket full of fresh Gulf Coast delicacies. The men had set everything up and watched the projector until he'd arrived.

She clutched a hand to her mouth. "What? You went to all this trouble for me?"

I'd do anything for you to give us a chance. "I thought you might find it romantic." She walked up to him, placing a hand on his cheek. He noticed a glaze of tears in her eyes.

"I find it extremely romantic." She kissed him softly, gently. He felt his breath catch. The need to hold her, to be close to her welled up in him. Without thinking, he wrapped her in a strong embrace, smoothing her hair. When he pulled away, he companionably caught her hand and led her to sheet covering the sand.

"Get comfortable," he said, smiling He set the picnic basket down in front of her. "I found a great local place, so we've got shrimp, fresh fruit and cheese, salad, lemonade, and some different po'boys in there."

Lila opened the basket, pulling out plates and cups. "You thought of everything." She placed the food out, so they could start fixing their plates. Grant moved over to the projector, tinkering with it until the screen lit up.

"I hope you like musicals." He watched her face as credits for Grease popped up.

"I love Grease!" She moved closer, handing him half of a shrimp po'boy. "I haven't seen this in forever."

"I thought about doing to something like Casablanca or An Affair to Remember, but for some reason, Grease kept popping my head. It's just fun. Plus, remember, Danny and Sandy got their start on the beach." He winked at her.

"Uh, huh...well, don't get any ideas over there." She winked back at him. They finished their dinner, then cuddled up together under the blanket. As the sky turned to night and Danny and Sandy found their way to true love, Grant wondered if they could do the same.

Lila woke up burning up. It took her a moment to realize it was because she was completely wrapped up in man. Squeezing her way out from under Grant's leg and arm that nearly pinned her down, she made her way to the shower. No morning sickness, she thought. *Gonna be a good day.*

A few moments later, Grant knocked on the door. She jumped at the knock.

"Come in," she yelled.

"Sorry to barge in on you, but Nick just called. He's got a

reporter tipped off that we are going to a place a few blocks down for breakfast so they can get some photos. Just wanted you to know before you got dressed."

"Glad you told me because I was planning to wear a big t-shirt and yoga pants for the ride home." She sighed, as she heard the door shut. Better play the part and look like a senator's wife. She finished her shower, then dressed in a white eyelet dress that was similar to one she saw Princess Kate wear recently and strappy nude heels.

In no time, they were at the restaurant ordering cinnamon buns and coffee. A thin man with even thinner hair approached them. "Mr. and Mrs. Harrington? I'm sorry to bother you, but I'm with the Ocean Springs Tribune and would love to take your picture for the paper."

Grant nodded. "Sure, we'd be glad for you to." They posed and chatted with the man. Easy enough, thought Lila. Could have been much worse. The photographer didn't take up much of their time. After another cup of coffee, they were loading back up in the car to actually head back to the Wisteria Inn, then home. *Home.* State College, Mississippi would be her home now. The thought made her nervous and jumpy.

Grant glanced over at her. "What are you thinking about over there?"

"Just about how we will be going to your house soon."

"Our house." He squeezed her leg. "It will be our house."

She stared out the window. *Yes, it will be. But will it ever be my home?*

11

Four hours later, they pulled up at the Wisteria Inn. Grant unloaded the car, while Lila eyed the bed longingly. The long car trip had her aching to stretch out in the bed and do nothing but watch tv and crash.

Grant set their bags down. "Oh, by the way, Nick set up an event for us at the local news channel here. They're calling it Meet the Harringtons."

"Meet the Harringtons? You didn't tell me about that." Fury was building in her chest. "You sure aren't' wasting any time getting in the photo op portion of our contract." She sighed. "We've been driving for hours, and you're just now telling me this?"

"I'm telling you now." He frowned at her, like he didn't see any problem with a pregnant woman getting ready for a public appearance after driving several hours. "I didn't think it would be a big deal. It's probably just going to be a some meet and greet at the studio that will air on the evening news."

"We've known each other for five minutes. We're

covering up a shotgun wedding and an accidental pregnancy. Did you not think for one second that maybe we need to work on concocting a story to tell the media? Maybe a little more than we met in the Bahamas and fell in love?" She threw her hands up. "What if they ask about our families? Our friends or hobbies? We don't know anything about each other."

He looked at her nervously, "I thought this would be good for us. It would give us a chance to get our story out there. Head off as much gossip as we can. When you start showing, we need to have already cemented ourselves as a loving, happy couple in the public's mind."

"Why don't we just announce we are expecting? This is the twenty-first century. We won't be run out of town." She was getting more irritated by the minute. *How dare he schedule something like this without talking to me?*

"I didn't..." Grant looked panicked. "Lila, I'm sorry. I've just been so worried about making sure we look like a legitimate couple."

Her anger simmered. *Is that what the night on the beach was?* There were no photographers there, she reminded herself. She sighed, trying to give him the benefit of the doubt. "I know you're trying. We both are. But we've got to be smart about these things. We're a team. We may not be anything else, but we are a team. You've got to keep me in the loop. And you can't make plans without me."

"You're right. I'm sorry. This is my first time having to run things by a wife." He smirked. She wanted to stay angry, but instead, smashed his face with her pillow.

"Well, consider this a fail." She grinned at him, pulling her blond hair back from her face. "We've got lots to do in a short amount of time. Lucky for you, I packed a few nice dresses, so I can wear one of those. I'm going to get a shower, take some more medicine, then we've got to review our story and get to know each other more. Fast. I'm not going to look like a fool on television."

She grabbed her clothes and retreated to the bathroom. With the water beating down on her skin, she was finally able to process their conversation. *Maybe this is how my mother has always felt. Like a pawn in someone else's game. Maybe that's why she's so bitter.*

She'd grown up seeing how her mother put on for her father. Always look perfect, be perfect, say the right thing, avoid scandal. Of course, in return her mother got to say she was Senator Hudson's wife. She was the queen bee in her social circle. She'd lunched with many First Ladies and even met a member or two of the royal family. But she was bitter. Delores Hudson was never satisfied. She'd always pushed Lila to do more, to be more. *Don't embarrass the family, Lila. Remember, you represent your father.*

Her father. Lila had a strange relationship with her father. At times, Ulysses Hudson could be kind and doting. He called her "Princess" when she was young and still occasionally used the pet name. She'd never wanted for anything and knew she could count on him to always be there.

The other side of the coin was her father was always "on." He was always worried about how things would be perceived by the public. He even planned things like family vacations around the media. Instead of looking for seclusion and privacy, he craved the media's attention and made sure they went to locations where the family could easily be photographed.

Lila dreamed of finding a kind, simple man to marry and love. Even though Kent had political ambitions, he never seemed as obsessed with politics as her father. Never in a million years did she dream their relationship was all part of some master plan he had devised to use her family name and her father's influence to achieve his own personal success.

She washed the last remnants of her peach shampoo away and applied a thin layer of conditioner. She went through the motions of shaving her legs and cleansing her body. *I'm doing what's best for my family. I'm saving my reputation and trying to do damage control after that mess Kent left me with. This is the best for everyone.*

She turned the water off and wrapped her hair up in a towel. She slipped on her robe then met Grant back in the bedroom. He was reading on his phone but stopped to look her up and down. She pulled the robe a little tighter. "Ok, I'm done. Hurry up and get your shower, so we can review our plan."

She dried her hair then curled it in soft waves. She applied her makeup a little heavier than normal, knowing she would need it to show up on television. She slipped on a navy shift dress with a thin cardigan and low-slung heels. She added her pearl earrings and an extra swipe of lipstick. She stared in the mirror, deciding she looked like a perfect political wife.

Grant emerged from the bathroom in his underwear. She tried not to stare at his muscular chest with its soft spattering of dark hair. He had a great body, she'd give him that. Long, lean muscles with a flat, ripped abdomen.

"How do I look?" She twirled around so he could see the full ensemble. He looked at her peculiarly, almost as if he didn't know what to say. He came over and stood right in front of her, resting his hands on her shoulders. She thought he might kiss her again. She tried to ignore the thought that a kiss wouldn't be too terrible.

"You look perfect. Classy and approachable." His eyes roved over her, dwelling a little too long on her slender legs.

"Thank you." Her mouth watered as she watched him dress in his charcoal gray suit. *Smoking hot.*

"So, we met in the Bahamas, whirlwind romance, couldn't wait any longer so we had the wedding here to keep it small and intimate?"

"Yep. If it comes up, I graduated from Yale with my doctorate in psychology. I've worked in D.C. as a professor at Georgetown for three years. Taught at Washington and Lee University for a year before that."

"Yale, huh? That's impressive. I went to Prescott University. The college in my hometown."

"Nothing wrong with that. So, you got your masters in accounting there?"

"Yep. Finished top of my class, then passed the CPA exams. After that, I worked five years at a local firm, Watkins, White, and Studdle. I left there to open my own practice, which I've maintained since then. Being mayor in a small town is actually a side job."

"I think it's great that you love your town so much. I can't wait to see it." She hoped he wasn't moving her to some backwards small town. "What about when they ask us what our families think of our marriage? Especially my dad?"

"We'll tell them our families were concerned, but they know how much we love each other and are supporting us one hundred percent. As for your dad, let's just say that he's getting to know me but supports our decisions."

"Ok, I guess you're right. I mean, we don't want to act like they just forgot that I was marrying someone else and got left at the altar."

"That's right. We've got to sell the lie, but in order to do that, we've got to believe it. And make sure our families are on board."

Before she knew it, they had changed clothes and headed to the interview. They pulled up at the studio and escorted into a small green room. A young intern brought them two steaming cups of coffee and instructed them to sit and relax for a few moments. *Live television.* She'd done this before. No need to be nervous, but she was. When they got the signal to head onto the set, Grant clasped her hand.

"Smile, honey. Just smile. It'll be fine." She plastered a fake smile on her face and walked out, hand in hand.

12

Grant looked over at Lila. She looked every bit the epitome of grace and style. He couldn't have picked a better political partner if he tried. She looked completely natural in front of the camera, which he assumed was from years of having a father in the political limelight. The newscaster, Bryant Griffin, greeted them, introducing Grant as the man who wanted to take Walter Henry's Senate seat.

Grant assumed the interview would be simple, down-home questions. He was caught completely off guard when Bryant drilled him on his political views, firing one question after another on political hot topics. He'd been under the impression this was going to be a human-interest piece.

He answered the questions the best he could, trying to sound calm and professional. Bryant turned to Lila. "So, Mrs. Harrington, tell us a little about yourself." If Lila was rattled at all, she didn't show it. She cleared her throat.

"Well, I'm from the great state of Virginia. I've lived in D.C. for the past few years and teach psychology at Georgetown University." She smiled coolly.

Bryant's eyes narrowed. "So, you recently met and

married? Can you tell us a little bit more about that? I'm sure the audience would love to know."

Lila squared her shoulders. *Here we go.* "We met in the Bahamas. I'd planned to just have a relaxing trip, nothing but tanning, reading, swimming..." She turned to Grant, sending him her most adoring look. "And then I saw him." She turned back to Bryant. "He just literally took my breath. I really didn't think the whole love at first sight thing was real, but boy..." She cleared her throat. "Let's just say, it's very real." She leveled her eyes squarely at Bryant. "It went from there. When it came time to go home, we knew we couldn't be apart. Not for one minute."

"We knew this was no ordinary romance," Grant interjected.

You can say that again, Lila thought. She placed her hand on Grant's arm, stroking his bicep. "So, long story short, he asked and I said yes. And here we are." Grant leaned over and gave her a soft kiss on the lips. She let her lips linger a beat too long, then grinned sheepishly at Bryant, giggling.

Bryant looked away momentarily and subtly nodded at one of the men standing to the side of the cameras. "Sounds like a whirlwind, alright. We've got time for one more question." He paused. "I hate to put you on the spot like this, but I'm just going to ask what everyone else's has been thinking." Lila felt her breath catch. "Is this just some move to try to get Senator Hudson to endorse you? Help win that Senate seat?"

Grant stared at Bryant. His jaw clenched. He fixed a calm smile on his handsome face. "Absolutely not. A man who will only marry for political reasons...well, that's a man who needs to check his moral compass."

Bryant looked skeptical. "Uh huh. Well, that's about all the time we have today. Thank you both for being on." The camera turned away, and someone yelled "That's a wrap."

They headed off stage, and Nick was already waiting at the entrance of the green room.

Nick's face was pinched. "That asshole Bryant...I think he's got connections with Henry. He was trying to trip you up and make your marriage look cheap."

Grant looped his arm around Lila's shoulders. "It's ok. Who's watching WBLT news anyways? Maybe a few folks around here?"

"Your constituents are watching, Grant. That's who."

Grant took a deep breath. "We'll talk about this in the morning." He gave Nick a pointed look before turning back to her. "It's fine, honey. No big deal." He held her hand as they walked to the car.

Her phone vibrated in her purse. She scrolled down the screen, reading the text. "Ummmm.... Grant? I think you might need to see this." Lila handed him her phone. "My dad just sent me that." Grant looked down to see a meme that someone had posted on social media. One side had a picture of them from the interview and the other side had a picture of Walter and Dolly Henry. It said WHO WOULD YOU TRUST? A MAN WHO'S BEEN MARRIED TWO MINUTES OR ONE WHO'S BEEN MARRIED FORTY YEARS? Comments under the image ranged from *Leave the Harrington's alone* to *He just got married to try to win. Some coincidence, huh?*

Grant handed Lila the phone back. "Let's just let it go. It's one measly interview. How much damage could it do?"

13

Lila watched as Grant ran his hands through his hair while pacing up and down the hall at the Wisteria. His phone was ringing off the hook. Nick had already called him three times, passing along the message that the local media was having a field day with Grant's "fake marriage."

She caught up to him in the hall and grabbed his arm. "Is it really that bad?" He looked like he was going to lie to ease her fears but must have decided against it.

"It's not good. Nick said people are sharing clips of the video from the interview all over social media. They're saying we look uncomfortable, fake, stiff. Some people are saying I hired you to marry me to help with the campaign." She averted her eyes. *If only they knew how right they were.*

"We knew this was a possibility. Guess we just have to deal with it."

"I don't really think it's that bad, but Senator Henry is an institution around here. Mississippi is often overlooked in the national spotlight, but he's been a long-standing fixture for us. People just love him. That's part of the reason they don't want to admit he's basically sat on his ass for the past decade, and let Mississippi fall by the wayside." Grant paced back and forth. "We need a lot of things to help us improve. The more you're here, the more you'll see it. Better schools, better access to healthcare, better health education. At one point, we were the fattest state in the nation with the highest rate of diabetes and teen pregnancy."

"So, do you think that's it? People just like him?"

"If you're not really paying attention, what's not to like? He looks like your ideal southern grandfather. He's been married for 40 years to the same woman. As far as I know there's never been any type of sex scandal. Or any scandal at all for that matter. He just doesn't do anything."

"My father's in the same boat. He's just popular and comfortable." She was interrupted by the ringing of his phone. Again.

"It's Nick." He rolled his eyes and answered the phone. He started pacing again. She heard him sigh. He was silent for a while. Then, his voice raised. It was the first time she'd ever heard him sound mad. "Yeah, I wanted to keep it quiet." Grant looked Lila up and down. "Okay that sounds good. We'll be here, so just text me when you're headed this way." He hung up the phone, turning it back on vibrate. "He's coming over to talk about everything."

"Good. Maybe he can help us smooth this out." She placed her hand on Grant's forearm. She stroked his arm lightly. It amazed her that her pulse quickened when she touched her husband. *Her off limits husband.*

"I sure hope so." Grant rolled his head back against his shoulders, trying to relieve some tension.

～

An hour later, Nick knocked on their room door. Lila couldn't help but notice how handsome he was. He wasn't that tall, maybe five ten or five eleven, but he was muscular with golden blonde hair and icy blue on ice eyes. With his golden skin and perfect teeth, Lila thought he looked like a Ken doll. He didn't waste any time. Without so much as a hello, he flopped himself down on the small sofa in the room, leaving Grant and Lila to sit on the bed.

"We've got to stop this mess. I've been thinking we need to come up with a few photo opportunities to make you guys look more like a real couple."

Lila sighed. "We are real couple. And we've already taken several photos."

"I know you are, but we got to prove it to the media. There is no comparison to Henry at this point, but our best bet is to make you look young and in love. We need to sell your love story. We need people to invest in it and invest in you."

"How do we do that?" asked Grant. "We had a whirlwind courtship and wedding. We don't know every little detail about each other. So what? It doesn't mean this isn't real and we don't love each other." He looked over at Lila. She smiled at him, trying to look like the confident, in love wife she was supposed to be.

"I'm happy for y'all. Really, I am." He turned to Grant. "You know you're one of my best friends. That's a lot of the reason I'm running this campaign. We were a long shot anyway, but I believe in you. I still do. We've just got to spin this in our favor." Nick pulled out his phone and flipped through his calendar. "I think we should plan an intimate dinner for tonight. I'll tip off the media that you'll be eating a Ginno's downtown."

"Do you think they will come?" She wasn't sure if they were important enough that reporters would spend their evenings taking pictures of them eating dinner.

"Oh, they'll come. Don't you worry. The main thing you need to concern yourselves with is looking blissfully. I want lots of PDA. But make it sweet PDA. Not trashy, like you are trying too hard."

Grant laughed. "So don't' stick my hand down her dress over appetizers?" Nick looked Lila up and down, causing her to blush. "Hey, man! That was a joke. Don't look at my wife like that." Grant punched Nick playfully in the arm. She liked the way "my wife" sounded. Even if the words really didn't mean anything.

~

She was thankful she'd packed a few dresses for their stay at the Wisteria Inn. She chose a plum cocktail dress with nude heels. She swept her hair up in a loose up do. Grant was dressed in dark dress pants with a light blue long sleeve button up shirt. His cologne smelled like sandalwood and made her think of their first night together. The thought sent a shiver down her spine.

Grant held the car door open for her. This time, he was driving them himself. The restaurant was only a few miles away, but he pulled over at a parking lot a few feet away from the restaurant. He unbuckled his seat belt and turned toward her. "I wanted to get you something before the wedding. Some type of gift, but nothing I found seemed like the right thing. While you were getting ready, I took a walk downtown. I spotted these and thought you might like them."

He handed her a small burgundy velvet box. When she opened it, a dainty pair of opal and diamond chandelier earrings greeted her, twinkling in the streetlight. She gasped.

"Oh Grant, I love them. They're gorgeous. Thank you so much." The thoughtful gift pulled at her heartstrings. She felt an unfamiliar fear well up in her chest again. *Watch it, Lila. This is just temporary.*

"I'm so glad that you like them. Thank you for putting up with all this. I know it's stressful, and I want you to know I appreciate it. And you."

"It's part of the bargain, right?" She laughed a little, trying to take the edge of her words. The feeling in her chest had her clipping her words. She pulled off her earrings, replacing them with the opals. She looked in the rearview mirror. They looked like tiny moon drops. Stunning. "They are absolutely beautiful." She softly kissed his cheek. "Thank you."

Grant's dark eyes looked deeply into hers. "You're welcome." He leaned over. His mouth was inches from her. At that moment, she didn't care about their deal. She leaned over, pressing her mouth to his. His lips brushed hers softly, then harder, as her mouth opened slightly. His tongue danced with hers, causing her blood to boil. She slipped her fingers through his dark hair, remotely aware that he'd unhooked her seatbelt. Before she could even think, she was crawling over to him, while he pushed the car seat back. She kicked her nude pumps off, letting them drop to the floor. His lips teased, driving her wild. She wanted him right then. To hell with their agreement. She reached for his shirt, when he grabbed her wrists. "Lila...Lila. I'm sorry."

"Don't be sorry." She reached for him again. She felt as if she might almost explode. Her mouth ran up the side of his neck, nipping his ear. He moaned. He grabbed her arms, pushing her back.

"Honey, I want you, too. But..." He looked around. "We're in the middle of town. That's the last thing we need is to get caught...well, you know. We could go to jail." Blood finally started to return to her head.

"You're right." She flopped back in her seat, trying to calm her racing heart. She flipped open the mirror on the sun visor. She wiped at her smeared lipstick and tried to straighten her ruffled hair. She slipped on her shoes. Crimson flooded her face. "I guess we better get to this then?"

Grant didn't say anything. He leaned over and kissed her quickly on the mouth. He straightened his shirt, trying to smooth the wrinkles she'd made from tackling him.

Lila took a deep breath, trying to steady herself. Grant got out of the car, then opened her door. He placed his arm around her waist, gently guiding her into the restaurant. "This is one of my favorite restaurants in the Delta. I hope you like it."

"I'm starving." She was led into a small, dimly lit restaurant with small round tables covered with white table clothes. Blues played softly in the background. Candles flickered on each table. The hostess guided them a corner booth, then a waitress came to take their drink and appetizer order.

When the waitress brought the succulent shrimp in Ginno's famous shrimp sauce to the table, Lila reached over to fill her plate. She noticed a man with a small black bag sitting in the corner of the restaurant.

She leaned over toward Grant, carefully not to brush her hair against the candle. Out of the corner of her eye, she saw the man snap a picture. "Grant," she whispered. We've got some action to my right." Grant sipped his drink and smiled like he was listening to a lover's secret. He reached over and ran his hand up and down her arm, then reaching for her hand. He held it there on the table for a minute, while she beamed up at him. "How are we doing?"

He slid closer to her in the booth and leaned over to whisper in her ear. His breath tickled, sending chills down her arms. "Just perfect. All we have to do is smile and look happy." The waitress returned, and they placed their orders.

"So, husband, tell me a little more about your family? I know you and your dad are really close, but you haven't mention much about your mom other than she divorced your father when you were younger." Grant's eyes turned hard, looking like molten coals. "Or, I mean, uh…you don't have to talk about it. I'm sorry if that's too personal."

Grant cleared his throat. She could tell he was trying to control his emotions. "You're my wife, Lila. No matter how that came to be, you are. I won't keep secrets from you." Lila was surprised to hear that but valued his honesty. "My mother left when I was nine. She just never came back. Sent my dad some divorce papers and that was it. No real explanation for either of us other than she needed to be happy. California made her happy. Apparently, we didn't."

"Oh, I am so sorry. That's just horrible. I'm sure that was so hard for you."

"I cried myself to sleep every night for a year." Lila's heart broke for the little boy he'd been. Grant looked troubled. "You know, I've never told anyone that. Not even my dad."

Lila ran her hand over her arm. She felt like she was walking a fine line. "I'm glad you told me. And I'm so sorry you had to go through that. Is that why you are so adamant of being here for …" She trailed off, looking down at her stomach.

"Yeah, that's part of it." He lowered his voice. "I don't ever want my child to feel that kind of pain. Plus, I grew up with a wonderful example of a father, and I want to be like my dad." Lila felt emotion welling up in her throat. *Isn't that what she always wanted? A man who would love their family, love their child, love her?* She knew without a doubt Grant would love this baby. She just had to wrap her head around that fact that he wouldn't love her.

She started to say more, but the waitress brought their food and placed it in front of them. Everything looked delicious. Grant dug into his steak, as Lila started to try a bite of her fish. It was seasoned perfectly and cooked so it was light and flaky. The first few bites were heaven. The more she sat there though, the more her stomach started to do flip flops. It was like the morning sickness but at night. She'd never experienced that before. She drank some of her water thinking it would pass. The wave of nausea started to build, higher and higher.

"Lila? Are you ok?" Grant sat down his fork and touched her shoulder.

"I don't think so. I've got to go to the bathroom." She stood quickly. Grant came around the booth, trying to escort her. "Grant, I got it…please…" She gripped the table. She thought she might pass out.

"Ok, just let me walk with you." He looped his arm around her waist, half carrying her to the bathroom. She saw the reporter stand up and aim his camera at them. If she hadn't been so worried about making it to the restroom, she would have confronted the asshole. A waiter, who was carrying a plate of steaming hot pasta, passed by, pausing to ask if they needed help. Grant said something but she couldn't hear it. All she could smell was the onions. They must have put a pound of onions in that pasta. Her stomach rolled. She felt the room spin.

"Grant…" She murmured, then suddenly vomited violently. She dropped to her knees. She felt hot, so hot, and then ice cold. Sweat beaded on her forehead. She was aware that Grant was beside her, trying to gather her up. The room spun again and faded to black.

"Call an ambulance! Lila, Lila…" She felt something cold on her head. The light blinded her as she fought to get out of the darkness.

"What?" She finally was able to look around. She was in Grant's arms sitting in the middle of the restaurant. Some man she didn't recognize in a dark gray shirt had his fingers against her neck. It took some time before she realized that he was checking her pulse. The whole incident came rushing back to her. She sat up, conscious that her dress was riding up her thigh. She tugged her dress down.

"I'm okay. Please don't call the ambulance."

Grant jumped to his feet. "If you don't get that camera out of here, I'm going to shove it down your throat. Have some respect." Lila realized then the reporter captured the whole thing on camera. The reported they had tipped off to be there. Her head spun again.

"Grant, I just want to get home. Ok? Please?" She realized when she said home, she was referring to her house in D.C., not the little inn.

"Are you sure we don't need to go to the hospital?" Fear was etched all over his handsome face.

"Help me get up and get to the bathroom, ok?" Grant lifted her to her feet like she weighed no more than a feather. Grant turned to the man in the gray shirt.

"Thank you for your help. I think she's alright." They walked slowly to the women's restroom, where she thought he would leave her to go inside.

"Who was that man?"

"He's a registered nurse and came over to make sure you didn't need CPR." Lila was mortified. "Oh God, Grant. I'm so sorry. This is so embarrassing. I haven't gotten sick at night before. It usually hits in the morning and resolves in a few hours."

"I really think we need to go to the hospital."

"No, it's passing."

Grant rubbed her back. "We are going back to the Wisteria tonight, but first thing tomorrow, we are going home." He kissed the top of her head. "To our home." She hadn't even seen his house yet. *Their house.* She didn't have the energy to argue or ask any questions.

Before she knew it, Grant got her loaded in the car and back in bed at the Wisteria. Tears were threatening to fall, just because she felt so weak and queasy. Grant helped her put on her pajamas, undressing her with quick efficiency. There was no lustful touches or kisses. All business. Once she was settled in bed, he left for a few moments and returned with several lemon lime sodas from the vending machine. The icy cold soda seemed to burn all the way down her esophagus and into her stomach, but it helped.

Grant took the drink and set it on the bedside table. He curled his long body around her, pressing his cheek to hers. The intimate gesture undid her. She started to cry, softly at first then with more force. He just held her tighter, allowing the storm to pass. Once she'd cried it out, he stroked her back in soft, rhythmic circles. She felt cozy, warm, safe. "You scared the hell out of me tonight," he whispered.

"I'm sorry," she whispered back. "I didn't mean to."

"I know you didn't." He ran his fingers across her hair, then kissed her on top of the head. "Tomorrow, we are going to the doctor. I can pull some strings in State College. I'm friends with a doc at church who delivers babies. They say he's the best in town. He'll see you tomorrow." She wanted to argue, tell him she would pick out her own doctor after doing research. Her stomach rolled again.

"Yes sir," she said sarcastically but pulled his arms tighter around her.

"There's something you should know." Her eyelids were getting heavier. "What happened between us...the way it happened...well, that's not something I do. Actually, I've never done. I think you should know that. I've had girl-friends but never met a woman and..." His voice trailed off.

"Had sex with her the first night?" Lila was too tired to have this conversation but somehow felt like he needed to say the words.

"Yes. I'm not that type of guy. I didn't know what to do the next morning. I've thought about you a lot since that night." She wanted to say she'd thought about him too. She wanted to say a lot of things. Then she remembered their agreement. *This is about his future and the baby*

She snuggled closer but didn't reply. His lips brushed her cheek. As she finally dozed off to sleep, a voice inside her head reminded her that Grant would never love her. She was his political partner, nothing more.

14

Grant woke up with his arm going numb. He still wasn't used to Lila being there. He tried to wedge his arm out from under her without waking her. She'd scared him to death the night before. He still wished they gone to the hospital. His phone buzzed on the bedside table. *Nick*. He picked up the phone, pulled on a shirt, and headed for the hall. He dreaded this conversation.

"Hello?"

"Why did you not call me last night? You are making my job impossible lately! I get a call that photos of Lila are plastered all over *The Jackson Gazette* this morning. The headline is "Bug or Bun." You better get tell me if I have anything I need to worry about."

Grant felt sick. *Lila is going to be mortified.* "I'm going to kill that bastard reporter. Who the hell prints photos like that? Does he not have any respect?"

"You're talking about the media. They don't respect anyone. Not even themselves." Nick paused. "Look, this is my job. You've got to trust me. Let me in on things, or I can't protect you. Was it the food? Or am I going to have more questions to answer about this nine months from now?"

Lila stuck her head out the door. "Everything ok?" She looked tired, all pale and dark circles under her eyes.

"Look, Nick, Lila just got up. Let me check on her, and I'll call you back." He hung up without giving Nick a chance to respond. He knew he'd hear about that later. Lila looked at him questioningly. He walked back inside, and they both sat on the small sofa.

Grant rubbed her back. "How do you feel this morning?"

"A little better. I'm actually not nauseated now. Maybe I got it all up last night." She held up a can of soda that had been on the night stand. "This helps. Thanks."

He smiled. "My dad always gave me ice cold Sprite or 7 Up when I was sick. Thought it might help a little."

She pointed to the phone. "What was that about? You look pissed." Grant gave her the rundown of their conversation. "Are you serious? That jerk printed the photos?" Her face was blood red. "You wait, I'm going to call that editor myself and let him have a piece of my mind."

"We've got to decide what we are going to do. People are really talking now, if they weren't' already. I think it may be better to head off the pregnancy rumors now."

"I just can't deal with this right now. Let's get packed and get on the road. We can talk about it then."

He knew Nick wanted an answer now. Grant turned his phone off. "Why don't you shower first? I'll start packing." As she retreated to the bathroom, his mind raced. *What would this do to the campaign?*

～

She dressed and packed quickly. Just in case a reporter was in the bushes somewhere, she'd taken some time fixing her hair and makeup. She slipped on a simple green cardigan with a thin cream blouse and dark skinny jeans with boots. She'd just gotten settled in Grant's Toyota 4-Runner when her phone rang. *Mother.* She debated on muting the call but knew Delores would never let up.

"Hello."

"Lila! Lila, oh thank God, you answered the phone. I've been getting calls. My friends, your father, now Bruce." *Not Bruce.* Bruce was her father's most trusted friend and advisor. He was also Senator Hudson's campaign manager every six years. Lila could only imagine what Bruce had to say about the headlines.

"Look, Mother. I'm sick. That's all. I don't know if it was the food or what."

"Well, it was embarrassment to you and this family. Do you know what they are saying about you?" Lila held the phone away from her ear, taking deep breaths. Grant squeezed her knee.

"No, I haven't heard. What exactly are they saying?" She paused, venom seething out. "That Senator Ulysses Hudson might have a blemish on his perfect record by that impulsive daughter who had a shotgun wedding?"

"Well, it's true. You didn't think people would talk? You were engaged to Kent. He was perfect for you. Perfect for us." Lila thought her head would literally explode. Nausea crept up in her belly again. She rolled the window down, in case she vomited. The wave passed. Apparently Baby Harrington wasn't too happy with his grandmother at that moment either.

Lila gritted her teeth, then took a deep breath. "Here's a newsflash, Mother. Kent was an asshole. A lying, two-faced, gold digging asshole. So, if that's what you want for your daughter, then you almost got it. Thankfully, he made one good decision in his life and that was to tell me the truth." She glanced at Grant. "And as for my shotgun wedding, Grant has more integrity in his pinky finger than Kent has in his whole body." She looked over at Grant again. He looked shocked but pleased.

"If you have any sense, you would learn how to be a good political wife. Keep your head high, your nose clean. Don't get fat. Don't sleep around. And for God's sake, don't vomit all over yourself in a public place." Delores sighed. "Get out there with him, smile, and shake hands. Show up that old, crotchety Dolly Henry."

Lila took a deep breath. "I really must go." She paused. "Oh, and Mother? I'm fine, you know. My husband took good care of me. I didn't go to the ER, even though we thought about it. Thanks for asking." She hung up and resisted the urge to sling the phone out the window. As she sat there trying to calm herself down, she was ashamed to think her mother might be right. *I've embarrassed myself, my family, even Grant. I should have known I couldn't do this.*

The two-hour drive back to State College passed in a blur. They stopped for lunch at The Ruby Grill, where she ate the best cream of chicken soup she'd ever had. She'd been nervous, but her stomach seemed to have settled down from the night before.

As they approached her new home, she was impressed by the rolling green hills of the countryside. Grant exited off the highway, driving them into downtown State College. They hit Main Street, and despite the circumstances, Lila felt her curiosity bloom. There was a charming bookstore and café. She saw the library, several clothing boutiques, a gift store, and three restaurants. There was also a small building with a sign reading "Magnolia Gallery."

"Is that an art gallery?"

"Yeah, it's been there a couple of years now. Mrs. Mauldin owns it and loves to showcase local talent." He gave her a sidelong glance. "Maybe you should think about taking your paintings?"

"If my own parents hate my paintings, why would anyone else want to see my art?"

"You never know. Just think about it. Mrs. Mauldin might need some help down there, if you miss working."

It seemed like she was always working, studying, or working on those incessant research papers with her colleagues. Suddenly, the idea of being jobless in a small town didn't sound so bad. "That actually sounds like a fun idea. Maybe she could use some help a few days a week." She twisted a piece of hair around her fingers. "I'll miss the security of my job, but I won't miss the actual job one bit."

"You don't have to work. I'm going to take care of you. Just thought it might be a way for you to meet people and keep you from getting lonely."

Without thinking, she squeezed his hand. "That's very thoughtful. Thank you."

He smiled at her. For a moment, she remembered that same smile from their first night at the Wisteria. That was the same smile that got her in this predicament in the first place. "So, what else do I need to know about my new town?"

"Well, let's see. We're a college town. You'll be surprised how packed this little place can get during football season. SEC football is huge. We tailgate, have watch parties, the whole nine yards."

"Tailgate?"

"People set up tents around the outside of the football stadium and have tons of food and alcohol. You just hang out at your tent or go from tent to tent visiting friends."

Lila patted her still flat stomach. "Sounds like fun, but I

think most of that will have to wait for next season." As soon as she said the words, she froze. That would be another whole year from now. She would either be a senator's wife or a divorcee.

Grant didn't say much for a few minutes, but he perked up when they turned off Main Street on to a quiet little street. They pulled up to a small brick bungalow style home with a huge magnolia tree in the front yard.

"Welcome home." He parked in the covered garage and helped her unload her bags. She walked in the house to see a cozy living room with overstuffed sofas and a fireplace. The house was immaculate and smelled fresh. "Looks like Dessie came today."

"Dessie?"

"My cleaning lady. She's a sweet lady from my church who makes a little extra spending money cleaning a few houses around town. She's worth every penny." He frowned. "Of course, if you don't want her to come…"

"No, of course I want her." Lila patted her flat stomach. "A pregnant girl isn't turning down any help." She giggled, then realized that was the first time she'd referred to herself as being pregnant without being upset or ashamed.

"Glad that's settled." He led her to a large bedroom. "This is my room. There are two other smaller bedrooms. I use one for an office, but I thought we could make the other one the baby room. And well, if you don't want to stay here with me, you could use the other." His brow furrowed. "I don't want you to feel uncomfortable in your own home."

He surprised her. His thoughtfulness tugged at her heart. She touched his shoulder briefly. "We're married. It may not be how I would have imagined it, but we will share a bedroom." She paused. "What if someone came by and realized we weren't staying in the same bedroom? The gig would be up."

"I hadn't thought of that. Good point." He laid her suit-cases in the floor. "You take all the time you need getting things set up and if you need me, let me know. I'm going to run to Dad's to get the mail."

Lila pulled open her suitcase and began putting away her clothes. Once she finished, she walked around the house, trying to picture what it would be like to live there as a real newlywed couple in love.

15

Her mother's words still burned in her ears. As much as Lila hated to admit it, she knew Delores was right. She needed to get out there with Grant. *Campaign, work.* She made up her mind. When she heard Grant coming out of the shower, she met him in the doorway. His towel was slung low over his hips. His wet hair stuck up from where he'd ruffled it with the towel.

"I want to campaign together." Lila paced back and forth the bedroom. Grant looked at her doubtfully.

"Campaign together? Are you sure?" He pulled open the dresser drawer, picking up a pair of boxers and a white t-shirt.

"I'm just as much a part of this you are. Ever since, well, ever since I agreed to marry you, I'm in this. That's why we got married in the first place, right? Help you win this race and help me not look like a loser. We need to win. I'll do whatever it takes to make us look like a loving, happy couple and ward off any gossip about this baby." She ran a hand over her stomach.

Grant dropped the towel. She tried not to stare, but

couldn't help but let her eyes wander. Her heart rate sped up as she soaked in his smooth, tan skin, flat abs, and muscular thighs. He turned slightly to step into his boxers. She bit her lip.

He noticed she was watching him and gave a devilish grin. "You know, you could help me dry off my back." He tossed the towel at her.

She rolled her eyes and threw it back at him. "Would you focus?"

He chuckled. "I am focused. So, what do you suggest we do?"

"I think we need a press conference. We admit we got married fast because of our whirlwind romance and pregnancy. We don't have to say a due date. It's nobody's business. And let's be honest, nowadays it's not that unusual for people to get pregnant before marriage. We can leave the public guessing."

Grant wrung his hands. "Okay, I'll call Nick. If we don't keep him in the loop, he's going to harass me to no end. I'll just tell him the truth."

Lila really didn't like the idea of anybody else being in on their secret, but she knew it needed to be done. "Alright, tell him." She ran a hand over her hair. "I've got to work on myself. I know I look a mess, and I'm tired of hiding that I'm sick. I think we just say that the episode at the restaurant was exactly what it was." She paused. "Surely people sympathize with a sick pregnant woman?" Sharp pain hit her abdomen. She clutched her stomach, waiting for the pain to pass.

Grant jumped up off the couch and rushed over to her. "Are you okay?" She took a deep breath. The room started to go dark on the edges. She shut her eyes, taking another deep breath. The dizziness started to fade.

"Yes, I don't really know what that was. I've had these sharp pains that hit suddenly but then go away. They almost take my breath away." Grant gathered her in his arms, stroking her back softly.

"I'm worried about you. I told you that I could get my doctor friend to see you."

"No, I want to pick my own doctor. I looked online and saw a women's clinic that's only a few miles away, so that will work out perfectly."

"Well, don't wait too long." He pushed her hair back from her face. "I want you and the baby taken care of." Grant looked deeply into her blue eyes. He looked as if he wanted to say something but instead pressed his lips against hers, catching her off guard. Her body quickly responded. His lips moved smoothly softly and then more urgently. Before she could even think about it, she wound her hands in his hair and allowed the kiss to go on and on.

When he finally pulled away, they both gaped at each other in shock. She ran her hands over the front of her pajamas, trying to appear as if she wasn't shaken. "Well I guess I need to get dressed, and you need to call Nick."

"What?" He looked confused. "Nick? Oh, yeah. Um, ok, yeah, I'll call him." He turned and walked back toward his office. When he was out of her sight, she finally let out a deep breath, trying to steady herself. If she was going to make this marriage work, she couldn't fall for her husband.

16

April 20, 2014

"Lila Hud-I mean, Harrington." Thankfully, she'd brought her new driver's license that showed her new name. The receptionist at State College OB-GYN Associates accepted the ID, then handed her a mountain of paperwork to fill out. She sat on the overstuffed couch in the waiting room, trying to calm her nerves.

Grant grimaced at the large pile of papers. "All that just to see the baby doctor?"

"Apparently so." She started answering the questionnaire the best she could and provided all her insurance information. It wasn't much longer before she was ushered into a small exam room. Grant looked nervous as a cat. He tried pacing in the small room but found that difficult given its size.

"What exactly are they going to do?" His dark eyes had circles underneath his bottom eyelids. She knew he'd been worried about the campaign and worried about her being sick.

"I don't know. This is my first time with this." She gave him a sad smile. "Remember, my first baby, too?"

Before he could respond, there was a knock on the door. Dr. Matt Graham was a tall, slender man with a shock of white hair. He looked to be in his early sixties and had dimples that popped out when he smiled. As he introduced himself and shook their hands, Lila found herself warming to him immediately.

Dr. Graham sat down on a stool in front of a small laptop. "It's so great to meet you both. I've looked over your history, Lila, and it looks like you are in great health. You're a healthy weight, have no significant medical history, and aren't taking in medication except Zofran, right?"

"Yes, sir. My doctor in D.C. gave me a prescription before I left."

"How is the Zofran working?" She wanted to lie and be brave but decided to be honest. Her mind flashed back to the dinner at Ginno's.

"I'm still getting sick. I vomit most mornings and have once or twice a night, too." Color flooded her cheeks.

"Hmmm, well, you are still in your first trimester, so nausea and vomiting is pretty common. I'm going to change you to Phenergan, and we will see if that will work better." He punched a few buttons on his laptop. "Done. Sent it to the pharmacy you have on file. So, basically what we are going to do today is first have an ultrasound to see if we can hear a heartbeat. You are nine weeks now, so we should be able to hear it. If everything looks good, then we will proceed with the physical exam and bloodwork."

If everything looks good? She hadn't thought of that. *What if the baby wasn't ok?* What if she'd miscarried? She hadn't seen any blood, but do people always have blood? She felt her pulse quicken. Dr. Graham led them to small room where the ultrasound tech greeted them.

"Is it ok if I stay?" Grant asked the tech.

"Of course, it is. We want you to see the baby, too, Daddy."

Grant's eyes widened. *Daddy*. She couldn't believe this man she'd only known for a short period of time was the father of her child. The tech, who introduced herself as a sonographer, explained that she was going insert a long probe in the vagina to get a picture of the baby. It wasn't painful, but it wasn't comfortable either. Grant looked like a deer in headlights. He seemed extremely uncomfortable during the process of starting the exam, but all awkwardness was gone when a loud whoop, whoop, whoop sound filled the room.

"That's him? Oh wow, that's our baby?" Grant asked.

"That's him. Or her. Way too early to tell. But the baby has a good strong heartbeat." The sonographer took several pictures then escorted them back to the exam room. After a few moments, Dr. Graham returned. Grant decided to duck out while Dr. Graham did the physical exam, and Lila was grateful. She didn't want to share a pap smear with anyone. Husband or no husband. A trip to the lab to draw what seemed like half the blood in her body, and they were headed back home.

They drove in silence. After a few minutes, Grant chuckled. Lila looked at him, eyebrows raised. "What?"

"Did you see the look on the doctor's face when you told him you were one hundred percent sure we conceived on Valentine's Day?"

"Well, I was. He kept trying to say estimated date of conception, and I was like, umm, no. I know when we had sex." She grinned. "I didn't want to bust you out and let him know you haven't been getting any."

"Well, I bet I'm not the only guy who gets his wife pregnant and gets cut off."

Lila laughed. It surprised her again how well they got along and how she was so glad he went with her. For a moment after the stick turned pink, she'd thought about not telling him about the baby. Keep things simple. But then she thought of the kind man who'd made her laugh that night at the bar when she'd been so sad, and she knew her conscience wouldn't let her. Not to mention having to explain why she'd done that to a child who would one day want to know their father. Seeing Grant in the doctor's office confirmed her decision. No matter what happened between them, their baby was going to have a loving father.

17

June 2014

Grant woke up to find Lila gone. He listened to see if she was in the bathroom, hoping she wasn't sick. The new medicine Dr. Graham prescribed seemed to be helping. He threw the sheet back, then pulled on a white cotton t-shirt. He padded down the hall to find Lila sitting up in the living room watching television.

Her hair was thrown up in a messy knot on top her head. She was wearing an old Garth Brooks concert t-shirt, which surprised him the first time he saw it. Then he found out she loved country music. It was nothing to come home from the office to hear Shania Twain or Conway Twitty blasting. Once he'd snuck up on her singing some Reba song at the top of her lungs and about given both of them a heart attack. He'd already bought tickets to see Faith Hill and Tim McGraw in concert in Tupelo to surprise her. She'd mentioned more than once that she always regretted missing their Soul2Soul II Tour when it came to Washington in 2006.

He peeped around the door. "Whatcha watching?"

She grinned and patted the couch. "Golden Girls. Never

gets old." He sat down beside her accepting half of the plush blanket she offered. She leaned against him as they watched Blanche and Dorothy argue over who was going to get to wear a dress to a dance. He laughed, enjoying the show and her. She felt so good curled up against him. He brushed his lips against her temple.

"You smell good."

She smiled up at him. "Thanks. I used your shampoo."

"No wonder I like it." He ruffled her hair. "What are you going to do today?"

"Been thinking about going to check out that art gallery you told me about in town."

"You should. Mrs. Mauldin is sweet, and I'm sure she would love to talk to you."

They finished the episode, then he got up and start banging around the kitchen. Lila sat where she was, curled up with the blanket. When he started pulling out all the ingredients to make biscuits, she came into the kitchen and sat down on one of the bar stools.

"How'd you learn to cook?"

He pursed his lips. "Dad taught me, I guess. Just seems like he was always cooking. I guess he had to when Mom left."

She looked down, then back up at him. "Do you ever talk to her? Your mother?"

He shook his head. "No. She left and never came back. Never called, wrote, nothing."

"How could she do that? I mean, the baby hasn't even gotten here and I would do anything for her."

"Her?"

"I feel like it's going to be a girl. Arabella Kate?"

"Hmmm... I do like that. Put it on the list. I think it's going to be a boy, but what do I know. Maybe Lawrence Grant?"

"And call him what? Wouldn't that get confusing with you and your dad? And quit trying to change the subject. Did she ever talk to your dad again?"

"She sent money for a while. He did tell me that. After three years of no contact other than a check, Dad told her to keep her money. He didn't tell me that until I was an adult. Basically, Dad had a booming local business, a name, and some money when they married. Business went south and he lost most of his money. So, she left and went and found someone else who had some."

"But your dad is very successful now, right?"

"Yeah, he built another business again from the ground up. He got his real estate license, started as an agent, then worked his way into having his own company. I never knew Mom's family. My grandparents died when I was a baby, and she only had one sibling- a brother who was killed in a car wreck when I was five. I vaguely remember Uncle Brian. Dad said he was a great guy. Was working his way through college when he was hit by a drunk driver."

Lila put her hand to her chest. "That so sad. How horrible to lose all your family like that."

"Yeah, it is sad. Dad thinks losing her family flipped a switch in Mom. She grew up without much money, but he swears when they married, she would have lived with him in a cardboard box. Somewhere along the line though, money and prestige became her idol."

"So, where is she now?"

"Last I could find on the internet, she married some movie exec out in Hollywood who is deliriously rich. He had two daughters, and there are pictures of her with them at their weddings. They made the society papers." He clenched his jaw, trying not to focus on how bitter that made him feel. "Anyways, when she left, Dad cooked. After a while, I started cooking.

He started mixing the flour, baking powder, salt, and shortening together. Lila watched attentively. "I want to learn. We always had a cook, so I never really learned. Although I loved to watch the cooks bake beautiful cakes and pies for Dad's dinner parties."

He was again reminded of how different their upbringings were. He remembered standing at the kitchen cabinets with Lawrence mixing flour, sugar, eggs, and milk in a big old green Pyrex bowl that had been Lawrence's mother's bowl.

As he stirred and poured, Lila chatted with him. Before too long, he pulled our fresh, hot biscuits that they ate with homemade strawberry jam courtesy of one of the little old ladies at church.

She bit into her biscuit. "These are delicious." Lila looked at the pile of dishes on the counter and in the sink. "I'll clean up."

He grinned devilishly. "Was hoping you'd say that." He stood up, pushing the barstool under the bar. "I've got a few meetings today but should be back after lunch."

"Ok. When I finish up here, I'm going to go to the gallery then run a few errands." Grant was glad he'd decided to go ahead and have her car sent down from D.C.

"You have fun. And talk to Mrs. Mauldin."

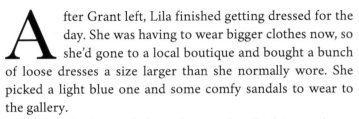

After Grant left, Lila finished getting dressed for the day. She was having to wear bigger clothes now, so she'd gone to a local boutique and bought a bunch of loose dresses a size larger than she normally wore. She picked a light blue one and some comfy sandals to wear to the gallery.

She made the quick drive there and walked in to a large,

beautiful building with brick walls in the entry. Statues and pottery sat on various shelves and tables. She stroked a brown and green bowl, which had been made locally. The edges of the bowl were ridged, and she could envision filling the bowl with mounds of apples and oranges. She checked the price tag. Forty dollars. That was a fair price. She picked up the bowl and kept walking.

A petite woman of about sixty came out from the back in a blaze of colors. She had red hair, several diamonds of all shapes and sizes adorning her neck, ears, and fingers, and a bright blue pant suit. A trail of gardenias seemed to linger in her wake. "Hello," she extended a small hand with perfectly manicured nails. "I'm Greta Mauldin. Welcome to my gallery."

Lila smiled, shaking the woman's hand. She absentmindedly placed her other hand on her abdomen. "Lila Harrington."

"Harrington. Are you Grant's wife?"

She blushed. *Was that a good thing or bad thing?* "Yes, that's me."

Greta lit up. "Oh, I just love Grant. He's my little sweetie pie. You'll never find better than that one."

"Well, thank you. I think I'll keep him." Taken aback by Greta's gushing, Lila felt herself relax. There would be no political discussions with this one.

"So, what brings you in today? That's one of my favorite pieces. Molly O'Bryan from down in Carthage made that. I can't seem to keep her pieces in stock."

"It's lovely. I'll take it." It'll be the first thing I buy for our house, she thought. *Our house.* The words still sounded foreign to her.

"Good. Now you just have a look around and let me know if you need anything. I'll go ahead and get that wrapped up for you." Greta took the bowl from her. Lila meandered around the building, stopping to admire several paintings.

Greta came back over after a while, watching quietly as Lila stared at a country scene oil painting. "I do rather like that one," Greta said.

Lila sighed. "I wish my paintings were that good." She checked the signature. "Whitney Brooke sure has a way with light."

"That she does," Greta said, peering over at Lila. "You paint?"

Lila could feel heat develop in her cheeks. "Yes, though nothing like this. I just...well, I paint for me. My mother wasted no time telling me they weren't good, so I keep them mainly at home or give them away to charities." She moved over twenty canvases with her to Mississippi, which were currently taking up residence in Grant's office.

"Bring them by."

"What?" Lila frowned.

Greta smiled. "I said bring them by. No reason for art to stay cooped up when it might could find a home some-where." She shrugged. "Now, I can't make any promises, but I might buy a few pieces from you." She pointed to a blank space on the white wall. "Got a couple of open spots."

"I couldn't. They're not any good. It's just something I do to kill time and relax."

"Why don't you let me be the judge of that?" She pointed to the register. "Come on, let's get you checked out so you can go get those for me before I close down today." Before she knew it, she'd somehow let Greta talk her into buying a large black and red Choctaw basket made from swamp cane and had her hauling all twenty-four paintings she had done back up to the gallery.

"These are lovely, Lila. Just lovely." Greta oohed and aahed over them, causing Lila to blush even more. She couldn't' believe the woman actually liked her paintings. Kent had always thought they were a messy distraction. Sophie encouraged her, but that was really the only person. *Had Grant known this? Had he known this woman would like her art?* Pride surged in her heart. He'd seen her paintings. They were in his office. He must have at least thought there might be a chance Greta would want them.

When it was all said and done, Greta chose six paintings to take to start with. Two were landscapes from a trip she'd made in college to Colorado, one was of the White House, and the other three were paintings of old churches and buildings she'd seen on various travels. "I'll give you four hundred dollars for the lot of them, and we can talk more once we see how they sell." Lila joyfully agreed. Headed home six paintings short and four hundred dollars richer, she couldn't have been happier.

18

July 5, 2014

Nerves rattled in Grant's body. He felt edgy, worried. Today was the day for the anatomy scan for the baby. He prayed everything would be fine. Lila seemed unaffected but for some reason, he was scared something would be wrong.

He showered and shaved, then slipped on a crisp suit. He had meetings later that day but wanted to be there for all of the appointments with the doctor. Heels clicked across the wood floor. He turned to see Lila standing there is a flowy blue dress. He let out a long whistle. "Someone is looking fine this morning."

Lila giggled. She looked him up and down. "Thank you. You look pretty fine yourself." Sometimes, he swore he saw desire in her eyes, but she'd kept up her end of the bargain and so had he. "I'm actually feeling a little better. That medicine Dr. Graham gave me helped.

"You've been eating better and seem like you have more energy."

"I do." She rubbed her hands together. "Once we find out what we're having today, I'm going to start working on the nursery.

As they drove the few miles to Dr. Graham's office, Grant tried to keep up the small talk. His mind raced, and he often couldn't keep up with the conversation. Lila must have noticed because when they pulled up at the office, she unbuckled her seat belt and turned to face him.

"Are you ok? You're acting weird." He debated on what to say to her. She seemed so happy. He didn't want to make her worry, too. He'd stayed up way too late the night before researching on the internet exactly what all Dr. Graham would check today. There were so many things that could go wrong. Sweat popped up on his brow. He turned the air up full blast. "Yeah, I'm fine. Just a big day." Lila frowned and stared at him for a moment.

"You're lying to me. Spill it."

He sighed. "Ok, ok. I'm just worried what all we will see today. What if…well, what if something is wrong?"

Lila pressed her lips together. "I've been trying not to think about that too much, but this morning I just decided that it doesn't matter. We will love our baby no matter what and will take good care of him or her." Grant reached for her hand, stroking the smooth skin. He didn't know how to ask what was really on his heart.

"Of course, we will. It's not that. It's just…Well, I mean…what if…"

"What if what?"

He stopped stroking her hand and looked her dead in the eye. "What if there's no heartbeat? I've read that it happens sometimes. I just don't know if I could handle that." He was shocked to feel hot tears trickle down his face. He wiped his face, embarrassed and ashamed.

Her blue eyes looked luminous against a sheen of fresh tears. She wrapped her arms around him, pulling him close. He ran a hand over her small belly bump. "I never thought I would have a baby, but now I can't picture not having one."

Lila placed her hands on top of his. "It's going to be alright. We have to believe that. Today, we will find out what we are having, then we can celebrate." She opened her car door. Before exiting the door, she turned to look at him. "You really need to be worried about how you are going to do all this campaigning and paint a nursery. Pregnant women like to nest you know." The question he couldn't voice still pinged in his head. *If something is wrong, will you leave?* Instead of asking, he smiled and opened his door. "That's why I have a campaign manager. Nick spent a few summers painting houses."

∼

The nurse led them into the chilly exam room. Goosebumps popped up on her skin as they waited on Dr. Graham. Lila mentally reminded herself to start bringing a sweater, even though it was smoldering hot outside. Humidity in Mississippi was no joke. She'd stop trying to straighten her hair and instead was letting it wave naturally before spraying layers of hair spray.

"Is he ever going to come? We've been in here for forty-five minutes." Grant unsuccessfully tried to pace up and down the small room. He could hardly take two steps without having to turn around.

"Maybe he's delivering a baby. Why don't you walk downstairs to the Coke machine and get something to drink?"

"No, I don't want to leave because then he'll come in." Grant seemed to get more irritated by the minute. She'd never seen him wound so tight, even with campaign. A warmth spread across her chest, filling her with a sensation she couldn't quite pinpoint. *He truly loves this baby.* Realizing that seemed to make the whole fake marriage almost worth it.

"Let's talk about names."

"I thought we wanted to wait until….. we knew everything was fine."

Lila took a deep breath. "Yes, but you're worried, and we aren't having bad juju going on before we find out all this fun stuff about our baby. So, you pick a first and middle name, then I will. You can pick either girl or boy, whichever. Go."

Grant hesitated. Lila slapped a hand on the exam table. "No thinking, Grant. Just say first thing that pops in your head."

"Ok. Nathan Andrew."

Lila nodded her head. "I like it. A lot actually." She whipped out her phone and punched a few buttons. "Adding it to my list. Ok, my turn. Isabella Sage."

"Isabella, yes. Sage, no. It's a cooking ingredient, Li."

She wrinkled her nose. "Fair enough." She raised her eyebrows, encouraging him to pick again. Grant rolled his eyes. "Umm, how about Jessica Rose?"

"Rose, yes. Jessica, no."

"What's wrong with Jessica?"

"Nothing's wrong with Jessica. It's a beautiful name. My father's side has a Jessica Anne, Jessica Leigh Ann, and Jessica Bailey. Too many Jessica's."

He laughed. "I agree. How about…" A knock on the door made both of them jump. Dr. Graham walked in, tablet in hand.

"Well, how are we today, Harringtons? Big day." He

scrolled down the tablet, nodding. "Yes, yes. Weight is looking better. Looks like we won't have to do the Reglan IV pump for now. How are you feeling?"

Lila chatted with the doctor about the last few weeks and before she knew it, he had sent them down the hall to the ultrasound room. The sonographer explained what exactly was going to happen. A few minutes later, they could see the baby on the screen. Grant clutched her hand tightly, squeezing it so hard she thought her fingers would snap. The baby's heartbeat filled the room. Grant finally smiled.

"See here, Mama? This is the heart." The sonographer clicked something that made a flashing sound, almost like a little camera. "I'm taking pictures of everything we need for Dr. Graham." She paused, wiggling the ultrasound probe. "I'm taking pictures of the heart, bladder, stomach, brain, and spine." She continued to work as they stared on in amazement.

Lila could see little hands but was mostly transfixed by the beating heart and the baby's small face. The sonographer grinned as she continued to snap pictures. "So, are wanting to know what we are having?"

"Yes!" Grant shouted. "I'm sorry." He dropped his voice. "I guess I'm just excited." That funny feeling filled Lila's heart again. He looked so eager and excited.

Lila giggled. "Yes, I think we want to know."

"Well…." The sonographer moved the little probe until there was a clear picture on the screen. Grant leaned forward, holding Lila's shoulder with one hand and squeezing her hand with the other. "Looks like it's a boy!"

Grant practically jumped on the bed with her. "A boy! Lila! I can't wait to call my dad." Grant brushed a hand over his face. Without thinking about it, she reached up and pulled him down to her for a quick kiss. The sonographer had turned her back to them, working on the computer. She glanced back over her shoulder.

"It's such an exciting day. I'm going to let you get ready then go back to your room. Dr. Graham will be in shortly."

After Lila got herself in order, they trekked back down the hall. She felt was now becoming familiar pressure in her lower abdomen. She looked up at Grant sheepishly. "You go in. I'll be there in a minute." After finding a bathroom, she peed for about the hundredth time that day. She admired the small belly bump, lovingly running her hands over her abdomen. *This is really happening. I'm going to be a mom.* She found the exam room and was surprised to see Dr. Graham already waiting on them.

She sat down beside Grant, instinctively reaching for his hand. Dr. Graham flipped through images on his tablet, nodding ever slightly.

"Well, good news. It looks like baby boy Harrington is in good shape. Heart, spine, brain, and all major organs look fine." He grinned at them. Grant buried his face in the side of her hair, laughing. She touched the side of his face, brushing his cheek with her lips.

"Love giving good news." Dr. Graham smiled. "Never gets old. So, I'll see you back in a month, but you make sure you keep yourself hydrated and call me if you start having any trouble." He patted Lila's knee and quietly stepped out. They went back to the lobby, set up the next appointment, and loaded back up in the car. It wasn't until they pulled out of the parking lot that Lila let out tears of joy.

19

October 2014

G rant looked down at his phone to see a text from Nick. *Turn on channel 3. Henry's ad on in five mins.* A few minutes later an ad showed Senator Henry wearing his Wrangler jeans and cowboy boots with his large cowboy hat perched on his head walking across his rolling hillside property. Another clip flashed to him with Dolly, then a picture of them on their wedding day filled the screen. Various members of his large extended family praised him as a down-home Mississippi boy with years of experience and polish, but also as a man who never forgot where he came from or who he represented.

"Great. That's just great." "How am I supposed to compete with him? Every time I turn around, all I hear is how he's been a senator forever, how he's got the perfect family..." He sighed. "I can't compete." He grabbed the phone, quickly calling Nick, who didn't answer.

"Calm down." Lila squeezed his arm softly. "Think about it for a minute. Why did you throw your hat in the ring anyway?" Grant sat there for a minute trying to think.

"I guess, I just wanted to see changes. I love Mississippi. I see all the things that need to be done, and I want to work to make it better. Henry hasn't done anything worthwhile in all these years."

"Well, then that's what you've got to remember. He has more experience. Ok, so what? What has he done besides spend time on Capitol Hill and earn a nice paycheck? Who cares how long he's been married? There are plenty of men in history who have done great things who were single. Or divorced. Or bad husbands. Who cares?" Lila paused.

"You know me, Lila. Or at least you're getting to know me. These other people don't. They think I'm just some young guy who wants to get famous or put myself in a good position to run for president one day. They don't realize that I have their best interest at heart."

He looked so frustrated, almost as if he was on the brink of tears. She started to go to him, but sharp pain hit her back, then radiated to the top of her legs, almost stealing her breath. Grant stood up quickly. "Are you okay?"

"I think…" she exhaled loudly, "I think it was just a cramp." She gingerly stood up straight for a moment. The pain eased up as she walked slowly over to him. She slipped her hand on top of his. "You're forgetting you have a great asset. I know this situation wasn't what you planned, but I grew up in the limelight. I grew up watching my father schmooze and make friends with all the right people in Washington. Henry may have more experience, but I can help you. We can do this together."

"I feel like Henry is all about himself. He's forgotten Mississippi. He's forgotten the struggling single mom on food stamps making minimum wage trying to make a life for herself and her children. He's forgotten about the once thriving Main Streets in our small towns that used to boom with business but now are rotting from neglect. Businesses are leaving or shutting down. As soon as kids graduate, they leave for bigger and better opportunities."

"Do you really think he doesn't care?"

"All I know is that he's hardly ever here and even when he is, it's usually for some big name event so he can get his face plastered all over the papers." Lila wanted to say something to help. Anything. She was surprised by the need to caress away the worry on his handsome face.

Without thinking, she reached for him. Pulling his head down to hers, her lips met his. The kiss was soft, hesitant, but then turned deeper, more urgent. She let him take her head in his hands and wind her blond hair around his hand as he pulled her closer.

She unbuttoned his shirt, exposing his tanned chest. He locked eyes with her, his dark brown eyes going almost coal black. His lips trailed down her neck, while his hands wandered lower to grasp her hips. He pulled back, looking at her questioningly. Without a word, she grasped his hand and led him into their bedroom. His hand slid under her loose dress and up her thigh, then danced over her belly, causing her to pull back slightly. She worried for a moment that he might find her body unattractive and pulled her dress back down.

"What's wrong?" he murmured against her shoulder.

"I..." she sighed as his mouth moved back up to the hollow of her collar bone. "You've only seen me naked once. What if..." She trailed off as he kissed her fully on the mouth.

"You are the most beautiful woman I've ever known. Then and now. Even more so now." He caressed the small belly bump gently. She could feel the tiny hairs on his knuckles brush against her skin, sending goosebumps down her spine.

She pulled him down to the bed and allowed herself to let go, giving into desire. If only for that night, he would really be her husband.

20

The sun streamed in through the window, startling Lila. She woke up disoriented. She looked over to see Grant sleeping naked beside her. Memories of the night before came flooding back. She couldn't help but smile as she remembered how tender and attentive he'd been. Always concerned about her pleasure, her comfort. She brushed his hair back off his face and pressed her lips to his forehead. He stirred, the opened his eyes gingerly against the sun.

Morning." He said gruffly. Without warning, he pulled her against him. "Turn over." Surprised, she turned on her side, so her bottom aligned directly up against him. He threw a leg over her, curling up tightly against her. His breath became even again, and Lila surprised herself by dozing back off, too.

"Lila." Someone was shaking her. She frowned. Opening one eye, she saw Grant, all fresh and showered staring back at her.

"It's almost ten o'clock, honey."

"Ten o'clock?" She looked at the bedside table. Grant kissed her softly.

"I got you something. Be right back." A few moments later, he returned with a large cookie sheet. "Hold this please." He left again and came out with a plate heaped full of bacon, scrambled eggs, and little tiny potatoes. A small bowl filled with strawberries precariously balanced on the side of the plate. He handed her the plate. "I don't have any fancy trays, so the cookie sheet will have to do." He helped her adjust so she could sit up in bed. Then, he brought in a steaming cup of coffee. "Put cream and sugar in it, just like you like it."

She marveled at his handy work. She'd never been much of a cook, and this breakfast looked delicious. "This looks wonderful." She scooped up some eggs and shoved them in her mouth. She stopped and stared up at him. She swallowed, then grinned up at him. "These are heavenly. What'd you add to them?"

"Lots of butter and goat cheese."

In no time, she'd woofed down the entire plate of food. She knew she needed to get up, but after such a full meal, all she really wanted to do was go back to sleep. She laid there for a moment, then tried stretching. A loud clap of thunder made her jump.

"It's supposed to be bad weather all day. We are under a thunderstorm warning and tornado watch." She must have looked alarmed because he continued on. "It just means conditions are conducive for a tornado, not that it will actually happen. I've got plenty of candles and snacks, plus lots of batteries for the weather radio. Even got some old rabbit ear antennas we can hook up for local TV, if the satellite goes out."

"So, what are we going to do all day?"

"Well, I was thinking if it was alright with you, we might just have a lazy, rainy day. I don't have any campaign stuff going on, and I already answered all of my emails. Nick is at his mother's house today for her birthday, so he will be occupied."

Lila looked at the fine specimen of a man standing in front of her. "I think that will be lovely." She settled against the pillows again. "I need a shower." She grimaced. "And to brush my teeth. It won't take five minutes. She pointed to his DVD collection against the wall. "Maybe pick a movie for us to watch?"

"Why don't you take your time in the shower, and I will wash up the dishes real fast. Then we can watch a movie?"

She nodded, grinning from ear to ear. She couldn't believe something as simple as a rainy day at home with her husband could make her so happy.

∽

Grant breathed in deeply. Lila smelled like honeysuckle. *Heavenly.* She dozed against his shoulder. He wiggled the fingers in his hand, trying to revive some feeling in them. They'd spent the whole day listening to rain, dozing, and watching movies. He couldn't remember the last time he'd been this lazy or content. As the day turned to night, they were on their third movie and had just finished a delicious dinner of homemade chicken stew, cornbread, and chocolate ice cream.

He'd always wanted someone to be like this with. Easy, slow, calming. He watched her breath in deeply, evenly. Her growing belly made his heart swell with pride and tenderness. As the last few scenes of the movie flashed across the screen, he felt his eyes drooping.

Just as he was dozing off, Lila's phone started to vibrate. She woke with a start. She grabbed the phone and answered quickly.

"Soph?" Her voice rasped. Grant moved his arm from out

from under her, allowing her to sit up in the bed. "Wait, ok. Hold on just a minute, ok?" She turned toward him. "I'm sorry. I'm going to take this outside."

"Sure, take your time." He pulled the comforter up tight, listening to the rain drip on the roof. He'd opened the window a crack, so they could hear the storm. The rain's pitter patter across the windows had his eyes falling again. All of a sudden, he could hear Lila talking. She must have walked out to the covered patio.

"I don't know, Soph. I miss D.C. I really do. You never know, I may move back sooner than you think." She paused. "He may not win." *Move back?* He sat up in the bed. *Was she planning on leaving him?* Even if he lost, she'd agreed to six months. He felt like he might vomit. *This is why I never let my guard down. Women leave if you aren't successful. They always leave.* He felt queasy and hot. *She'll leave just like Mom did.*

She breezed back in the room, her blond hair windblown. She crawled back in the bed. He moved away when her leg brushed his. She looked confused, but tried to move closer. He jerked away from her.

"I'm pretty tired. Think I'm about to call it a night." He knew his voice sounded clipped, but he couldn't stop thinking about what he'd heard. She must be thinking about leaving. *Hell, maybe she didn't even want to be here now.*

Lila looked taken aback by his tone. He tried to soften his voice. "Goodnight, Lila."

"Goodnight, Grant." She flipped the light off. Before she had time to try to curl up close to him, Grant turned his back to her and moved as far to the edge of the bed as possible.

21

Grant went back to the office to work on the points he wanted to make at the town hall debate that night. Irritation seethed under his skin. He felt edgy and irritable. He thought after the romantic night they'd shared that things were changing. That they might be a real couple, a real family. *Maybe Lila could really love me.* His mind kept wandering to his mother. *She didn't love me. If she did, she wouldn't have left. If my own mother couldn't stay, then why would Lila?* He rubbed his face. *Stop it. Mom made her decisions. Don't blame other people for them.*

If he could just get to this debate behind him, he'd focus on things with Lila. She was a good woman, and no matter what happened, she would always be the mother of his child. Even if she left. He tried to deal with the anxiety that crept up his chest, trying to decide if it was from the thoughts of Lila or the debate that would begin in a few hours.

~

Lila didn't know what was going on with Grant. They'd had a wonderful day and night together, talking, laughing, and being lazy. He'd been loving, affectionate, and kind. It seemed like when she got back in the house from talking to Sophie, he'd completely shut her out.

She'd worried he'd overheard her conversation with Sophie, but she knew he hadn't. He couldn't. She'd told Sophie about how much she'd enjoyed her cozy day at home with Grant. She'd giggled and told her that she was falling in love with Grant. Sophie had laughed and said don't you mean falling more in love. She'd caught herself and corrected her statement. Maybe he'd heard her say she loved him. Maybe that was what was freaking him out.

Sophie kept saying how much she'd missed her, so Lila assured her that she might be back in D.C. soon. She meant if Grant won. And if he didn't, well…. she'd be back in D.C. then, also.

The town hall debate was set to start at six o'clock that night. Grant arrived an hour early to give himself time to calm his nerves. He'd worn a new charcoal gray suit with a crisp red tie. Lila had on a fitted black dress and low-slung black heels. She styled her hair differently, in a loose knot on top of her head, showcasing the opal and diamond earrings he'd given her. She looked regal. While they were waiting in a small room before the debate, a tiny television in the corner of the room broadcasted the local news. Grant rehearsed his opening speech but was interrupted be the television's booming announcement. WANT TO SEE MISSISSIPPI FAIL? LOOK NO FURTHER THAN GRANT HARRINGTON.

Grant whipped his head up, just in time to see the montage of sound bites, unflattering photos, and a list of his shortcomings flash across the screen. Lila saw the ad, too. She looked at him and stroked his forearm. Her touch set his teeth on edge. He knew she didn't care about him. She was just biding time until she could leave. Grant brushed her hand off, trying to ignore the hurt in her eyes.

"Grant, are you alright?" Lila looked worried. She cupped her hand under her abdomen.

He shrugged his shoulders. Defeat rolled over him. *Who am I kidding? I'll never win this. And if I lose, she'll leave. I'll lose the race, Lila, and my baby.*

"Grant? Are you listening to me?"

"I heard you, Lila. I need some space, ok?"

She couldn't have looked more surprised than if he'd slapped her. "Space? Sure. Fine. I'll be in the hall. Come get me when we have to go put on the show."

The show. That's what it was to her. He knew better than to fall for her. She'd never want him, never see him as a success.

Not five minutes after she left, Nick knocked on the door. "Show time, brother." Grant paced the room a few times, trying to summon his courage. Nick had already gotten Lila to the stage door. In a matter of seconds, they'd crossed the threshold on to the stage, smiling and waving to the audience.

The moderator took a moment to introduce the opponents and their families to the crowd. Of course, Henry had pulled out all the stops, having all four children and his herd of grandchildren join him on the stage for the introduction.

As they began the debate, the hot lights of the stadium beat down on Grant. He tried to focus on the moderator and keep his answers short and direct. Let Henry bellow on about all his years of wasting tax payers' dollars. Grant tried to remind himself that he wanted to stand apart and show voters that he had a plan.

Grant tried to ignore the television cameras from the local station that were airing the debate live. They battled back and forth, question after question. Grant stumbled, often having to have the questions repeated, or taking so long to respond that his time ran out before he finished. He felt like his mind was made of mush. He kept thinking he was going to lose. Then Lila would leave. It played in his mind like a broken record.

The moderator led into what would be the last question. He asked both men to tell why they would be the man for the job. Senator Henry took the full allotted five minutes to list all his accomplishments, his love for Mississippi, his desire to make the state a better place for his grandchildren. Grant looked out over the crowd. They were eating it up. Eyes fixed, enthralled on the senior statesman, who looked the part of an accomplished politician. The highlight wheel of all his shortcomings from the ad he'd seen on TV flashed across his mind.

"And you, Mr. Harrington." The moderator's blindly white teeth flashed at him. "Why would you make the best senator for our fine state?"

His mind froze. *Why would I make the best senator? I'm not as accomplished. No way my resume holds up against Henry's. My marriage is a sham. Why would anyone trust me?*

"I….um…I." He felt dizzy and hot. "What…what was the question?" The moderator looked confused, but dutifully repeated the question. Slowly and carefully enunciating, as if Grant couldn't hear him well.

Grant looked in the audience making eye contact with Lila. She nodded and smiled. He took a deep breath. *Get it together, man.* "I love our state. I know my resume can't compare to Senator Henry's resume. But in my defense, he's got about 30 years on me. No offense, Senator Henry." The crowd chuckled. "I want to make a difference here. I want to try new things. I want to see our small, dying towns come back to life. I want Main Street to mean something again. I don't have all the answers. But I know doing the same old thing as we've been doing for the past decade isn't going to change anything." He breathed a sigh of relief and nodded at the moderator. Before he knew it, he'd shook hands with the moderator and Henry, then retreated to the small dressing room.

Nick bust into the room without knocking. He slapped Grant on the back. "I'm not going to lie, buddy. You didn't start strong, but I think you closed well. It was a good ending, maybe something to let the folks go home and chew on."

Grant buried his head in his hands. "Nick, I think it's over. I stunk tonight. I just can't seem to pull it together, get my thoughts out of my head clearly. I think we're done, man."

Nick stared at him, mouth open. He was silent for a minute, then slugged Grant in the shoulder, as only a best friend can do. "What the hell do you mean it's over? We haven't been working our asses off for the past two years building this campaign for you to throw in the towel before election night?" He clenched a hand at his temple. "What's wrong with you, man? This isn't like you."

Grant stared at his lifelong friend. Before he knew it, he poured the whole story out. When Lila knocked on the door, Nick politely asked for a few more minutes with his friend. They sat side by side on a bench in the dressing room.

Nick shook his head, staring at his hands. "Maybe you're reading her all wrong? She's been a trooper. I don't think she would just leave you like that."

Grant looked up at his friend. "She's going to leave if I don't win."

"Maybe she just meant if you didn't win, she would be back in six months, like your agreement said."

"No, I think if I lose, she'll leave right away. Contract or no contract. She doesn't really need the money. I'm sure her daddy has a nice big trust fund for her, if I had to guess."

"So, what are you going to do?"

"What do you mean do? What is there to do?"

Nick pursed his lips. "Come on, Grant. Think. You're married to the daughter of one of the most powerful men in the nation. *The nation.* Don't you think you could use that to your advantage? Get him down here stumping for you or something?"

He'd thought about it. More than once. His mind flashed back to Lila telling him about Kent. He'd always thought asking for her father's help would somehow be betraying her. But now that the fate of the race and their marriage hung in the balance, it almost seemed stupid to not involve his father in law.

"I guess I could call him. He gave me his number at the wedding, in case I ever needed anything."

Nick grinned. "Well, what are you waiting for? Call him."

22

The next morning Lila woke up to a knock on the door. Grant, who'd been distant all night, was in the shower. She almost dropped her steaming cup of coffee when she opened the door. The stern, knowing face of Ulysses Hudson stared back at her.

"Lila, dear." He looked smug.

"Father? What are you doing here?" Icy chills raced down her spine.

"Oh, you didn't know? Looks like my son in law finally came to his senses. He brought out the big guns. Cashing in on that good family name you have." Ulysses entered the house without waiting to be asked in.

"What? Grant…he did what?" She'd heard him. She just didn't want to believe it.

"He asked me to come help him. How could he lose with a name like Hudson linked to him? Finally woke up that he married a political darling." He pinched her cheek and winked. She fought the urge to slap him.

Anger boiled in her chest. Grant must have heard the

commotion, because he came in with just his jeans on and no shirt. She fought tears.

She glared at him. "You called my father? One bad debate and you called him?" The tears trickled down her face. Grant looked shocked.

"I just thought he could help." She held up a hand.

"I know exactly what you thought, Grant. Might as well cash in on your political cash cow."

"What? That's not what I thought at all. I just want to win."

"You just want to win?" She stared at him for a moment. Was he so stupid that he didn't realize he was using her just the way Kent had? "Well, I guess I must always pick the same type of man. Someone who is much more interested in my father than me." She grabbed her purse and tromped to the front door. "I'm leaving. Do whatever you want, but I'm not sticking around for this."

At least Ulysses had the good manners to look shocked. She slammed the door behind her and climbed into her car. Grant followed her outside.

"Lila. Open the door." He pounded on the window. "Open the damn door!" She looked at him, tears streaming down her face. Her belly poked against the steering wheel. She instinctively touched her abdomen.

"It's going to all be ok, sweet pea." She whispered to the baby. "It's going to be fine." She rolled the window down a crack. "Grant, get off the car. I'm leaving."

"You can't just leave. You are due any day now."

"I'll be just fine. Now, seriously, get the hell off my car." She whipped the car back. Once she'd gotten on the highway, she made the tearful call to Sophie.

23

Thank God for Sophie. When Lila called, Sophie boarded the first plane, since Lila couldn't fly so late in the pregnancy. Lila rented a room at the Wisteria Inn, but specifically requested a room furthest away from the one she'd shared with Grant. She didn't know why she was drawn there, but the inn made her feel safe and secure. Grant had called numerous times. She hadn't answered. She just couldn't.

Early the next morning, after a sleepless night, she pulled up to pick up Sophie at the airport. In her big sunglasses and oversized t-shirt, Sophie looked like an angel. Her angel. She hugged her best friend, squeezing her as tightly as she could with her large pregnant belly between them.

"It's so good to see you," Lila murmured against Sophie's hair, before she released her friend from the hug.

"I'm glad to see you, too." Sophie heaved her bags into the trunk of the small car. She slid in the passenger seat. They were quiet for a few moments. "Ok, spill it. What the hell's going on?"

Lila told Sophie the whole story, including the marriage contract. To her friend's credit, Sophie didn't condemn. She just listened. When Lila had finally finished the whole story, they'd pulled up at the Wisteria.

"Look, honey, we've got lots to discuss here. I'm going to need some caffeine, first." A quick call to room service and they had a steaming pot of hot coffee and some blueberry scones. Lila picked at a scone, while Sophie poured a huge mug of coffee.

She tentatively sipped the coffee, peering at Lila thoughtfully. "Now, that's more like it." Sophie pinched off a small piece of the scone and chewed. She closed her eyes for a moment, savoring the flavor of the scone. "These are wonderful." Another sip of coffee, then she cleared her throat. "Do I have friend privilege?"

Friend privilege was what they said when they wanted to say something they thought would be in the best interest of the other and as a best friend, they had the duty to say it, even if they knew it would hurt the other's feelings or make them mad. Friend privilege meant the other couldn't be mad.

"Yes, you have friend privilege." Lila leaned back against the headboard of the bed, waiting for the lecture.

"Do you love him? I mean, really love him? Because if you don't, screw it. We'll call the whole thing off."

Lila sighed. "Yes, I love him." She slung the throw pillow against the wall. "What's wrong with me, Soph? I know he doesn't love me."

"How do you know that? Why is it so impossible for you to believe that he could love you too?"

Lila's mind flashed back to him helping her when she was sick. Holding her. Making love to her. The tears she'd been fighting spilled down her cheeks. "I don't know. I guess…" She wiped her face with the Kleenex Sophie offered her. "I guess I just think about Kent. We'd known each other for years. I thought he really loved me. And it was all a lie." She lifted her bloodshot eyes to her friend. "How could Grant really love me when this has all been a lie from the beginning?"

Sophie raised her eyebrows and grinned. "Well, how can you?"

"How can I what?"

"How can you love him?" Sophie placed her hand on Lila's arm. "You both started at the same place, Li. You obviously had an instant attraction, but attraction isn't enough. It never is. It went deeper than that for you over time. Maybe it did for him, too." She glanced at Lila's phone, which had been turned on silent. "Look at your phone." The screen read 10 missed calls and 7 text messages. "If I'm guessing right, all of those are from your husband."

Husband. Even now, those words sounded so foreign. "So, what do I do?" She wrung her hands together. "I'm going to have to deal with him in some capacity for at least the next eighteen years." She rubbed her belly.

"Well, first of all, I think you need to get your head together." Sophie sighed, twisting her dark hair in a knot on top of her head. "Look, we've been best friends forever. I've tried to tell you this in a nice way, but I think you need a little tough love. You need to grow a pair regarding your parents. Who cares if your dad is some big fancy senator? You are a grown woman. Your life is your life, and you've got to quit making decisions based on what you think your parents want or how it looks to the media." Lila started to speak, but Sophie held up her hand. "I'm not done. Take a little responsibility. You and Kent were never truly happy. Maybe you didn't fight, but you never really seemed that into him."

Lila jerked her head back. "Into him? We were engaged!"

Sophie arched an eyebrow. "You and I both know you loved when he was out of town. You dreaded when came home." Lila frowned. *Had she?* She always loved to see him go so she would have time alone.

"From what you've told me, you and Grant have been stuck like glue. And you haven't seemed to mind it all."

Lila thought about it for a moment. She loved being with Grant. He was kind, fun, patient, and well, he felt like home. "I do love being with Grant. It's easy. Has been from the night I met him."

Sophie smiled. "Well, there you go. Now get a backbone. Tell your parents you're cutting the cord, tell Grant the truth, and let the chips fall where they may."

Just like that. Sophie always knew how to cut through the junk and get to the heart of the matter. Lila reached for friend, hugging her tight. "You're right. I know you're right. How about I go wash my face and let's go do some shopping? Maybe a little retail therapy will help me with my backbone? Then we can head back to State College. You can stay at the little B&B in town, then once I get this over with...well, if he loves me too, you're staying with us. If not, we're driving back to D.C."

"I'm not so sure your doctor would want you driving thirteen hours so late in pregnancy."

Lila furrowed her brow. "Well, let's hope Grant loves me, then."

24

Grant grimaced at the sound of the phone buzzing loudly on his nightstand. He slapped the phone, hoping to make the device ceases that incessant buzzing. What time was it anyway? He groggily looked at the bedside table to see the clock. 5:10 AM. He looked down at his phone, seeing a missed call from Nick. *What the does he want at this time of morning?* Sitting on the edge of the bed, he tried to clear the sleep from his eyes. He called Nick back.

"Morning, sunshine."

Grant sighed. "What is it?"

"I've got opportunity for you."

"An opportunity?"

"Yeah, I got a call last night about a chance to work with underprivileged kids in the Delta. They need some help building a playground and a pavilion at a local church. Plus, the kids need someone to spend time with them." Nick paused. "I thought it might be good for you. There's only one condition."

"What's that?"

"No publicity."

Grant mulled this over. He really did need to get away. Maybe doing something just for the sake of helping others would help him reconnect with the reason he was running for office. "Okay, I'll do it. When should I be there?"

"Well, that's the thing. They want to start work at seven this morning."

"Seven o'clock?" He glanced at the clock again. If he left now, he would barely make it in time.

"Get up and get moving."

"Whatever." Grant rolled his eyes and hung up.

After a quick shower, Grant pulled on an old T-shirt and jeans. He grabbed a jacket and a pair of work gloves. He jotted off a quick note to Lila telling her where he was going, in case she decided to come back.

When he pulled up in the sleepy small Delta town, he was surprised to see several men and women gathered working at the church. Children slowly starting to come out of their homes to see what the action was all about. Before he knew it, he was put to work building the walls for the pavilion. He spent the day talking to children, breaking his back lifting supplies, helping serve lunch, and playing with the kids on the old swing set that stood in the churchyard. He forgot all about campaigning and remembered why he wanted to do this job in the first place. He wanted to connect with the people of his state and make a difference.

L ila and Sophie spent the morning and first part of the afternoon shopping at the few high-end boutiques lining the small Main Street, eating Delta tamales, and even hit up the spa downtown. After a few hours with her friend, Lila's mood lifted. She was building up her courage for the discussions she'd have with her parents and Grant. She felt pain in her back but chalked it up to Braxton-Hicks contractions. She'd had several episodes of those before, and Dr. Graham told her they were nothing to worry about.

When they got back to the room, Lila laid down on the bed. She was so tired all of a sudden. Probably just from finally relaxing and all that walking, she thought. Sophie started packing. "I'll help in just a minute. I think I need to lay here for a moment." She felt dizzy. Shutting her eyes, she took deep breaths.

"Are you ok? Lila?" Sophie's voice echoed in her head. The wave of nausea hit her so forcibly, if she'd been standing, she might have fallen. The contraction started in her back but radiated to the front of her abdomen in swift, rolling pangs. She tried to sit down and see if that would help. The pangs kept on, rhythmically. She grabbed her stomach. *It's too soon.*

She sat up but that made it worse. She laid back against the cool pillowcase on the bed. Wave after wave of pain swamped her abdomen. Sophie was talking to her, but it was like she was listening underwater. The room started going black around the edges of her vision. She felt herself let go and drift into the darkness.

G rant was headed back from the Delta, enjoying the peaceful ride through the flat plains. His phone rang showing an unfamiliar number. He almost didn't answer thinking it might be some reporter. The phone kept ringing, so he finally gave in and answered.

"Hello?"

"Grant?"

"Yes? Who is…"

"This is Sophie. Look, Lila called me to come down here last night. We've been at the Wisteria. She seemed fine, but..." She started to sob.

Grant felt all the blood drain from his brain. "Lila...is she...The baby?" He couldn't seem to get his tongue to form words correctly. He swallowed again. "Are they ok?"

The other end of the phone was silent for a moment. "I don't know. They won't tell me anything since I'm not family. She passed out when we were at the inn..."

"Where are you?"

"Greenwood-Leflore Hospital. It's..."

"I know where it is." He checked the clock. "I'm not that far away. Should be able to be there in about fifteen minutes."

"Ok, I'm sorry. I wish I knew more."

Grant took a deep breath trying to push back the panic rising in his chest. He wanted to scream. But screaming wouldn't help anything and would upset Sophie. "Call me back if you find out anything else." He hung up the phone and turning on his emergency flashers. He watched as the speedometer rolled up to 70, 80, 85 mph. That was one good thing about a lonely, flat Delta highway. No one there to get in the way.

25

Grant burst through the doors of the hospital. He ran up to a receptionist who pointed him in the direction of labor and delivery. He found the small waiting room. There was one older couple, most likely expectant grandparents, carrying a large bouquet of flowers and bright pink balloons. Sophie was hunched over in the corner, all alone. They'd only met once before, but he rushed to her and enveloped her in a hug.

"Any word?"

"No. They asked who they needed to call. I told them I called you." She bit her lip. "Here I was giving Lila a pep talk on being brave, and I gave that innocent little nurse the job of calling her family. I just couldn't deal with Delores. Not right now." She sighed. "She was fine, Grant. We shopped, ate lunch. She was fine. Then she wasn't."

Grant squeezed her hand and went to the nurses' station. He asked about Lila and was told someone would be out to talk to him soon. He sat back down with Sophie.

"I should have called her parents. I should call my dad." Grant raked his hand through his hair. "I can't think." He pulled out his phone. He punched in a few numbers.

Moments later, his father was picking up Nick, and they were headed that way.

A thin, brunette nurse with big blue eyes approached them. She had on cheerful pink scrubs and a serious expression. "Mr. Harrington?"

Grant stood up and extended his hand. "Yes, yes. I'm Grant." She smiled. "I'm Liz. I'm one of the nurses taking care of your wife."

"How is she? Can I see her?"

"We're doing the best we can, sir. Your wife is having strong contractions that are very close together. We're trying to slow them down, to prevent stress on her and the baby."

He tried to process everything. The nurse kept talking. "If you'll come this way with me, we will get you gowned up."

"Wait, what?" There was a whirling noise in his head. He couldn't focus on what she was saying.

Liz patted his arm. "If we have to do a C-section. That way you can be with her. If it's emergent, you may have to stay behind."

He nodded dutifully. Next thing he knew, he was wearing a blue hospital gown, gloves, and a hair net. His hands shook. *Get it together, Harrington.* He took a deep breath, summoning his most calm, supportive face. Lila looked so small lying in the bed with all kinds of wires and machines hooked up to her.

"Hey, you." Her voice croaked. She picked up a small ice chip from a cup. "This is all I can have right now."

He sat down beside her and laid his head against her chest. He wanted to be calm, brave, a rock. But the tears started falling. She ran her hands through his hair, kissing his hair softly.

"I'm so sorry. I should have been there. I'm so sorry I called your father." It all seemed so pointless now. *What did the stupid race even matter?* He kissed her on the mouth.

"It's ok." She squeezed his hand. "We've got so much to talk about." The monitor beside the bed starting dinging. She closed her eyes and tried to breathe slowly through pursed lips.

"What's going on? Do I need to get someone?" He didn't have to. Liz, two other nurses, and an older woman wearing a white coat that said Dr. Donna Sullivan rushed into the room. They started unhooking wires and moving monitors. Someone pushed him back then pulled up the side rails on Lila's bed. He vaguely heard someone tell him they had to go and go now. He started running with them but was instructed to stay outside the big metal doors, as the medical team rushed ahead with Lila. He pulled on the doors, which were locked.

He leaned against the cold, white wall and allowed himself to slide down to the floor. Hands between his hands, he wept.

26

A few minutes later, though it seemed like an eternity, Liz appeared back outside. Grant jumped up from the floor.

"What's going on? Are they alright?"

"There's basically two problems. The baby's heart rate is decreasing, and Lila might be developing a condition called preeclampsia. We are prepping her for a cesarean delivery now. It may be an emergent delivery, so it's best if you stay here."

He couldn't believe what he was hearing. He wished they were at the hospital in State College with Dr. Graham. Dr. Graham would have made him feel better. He took a deep breath. "But they will be okay, right?"

The nurse was somber. "We will do the best we can. I'll be back out as soon as we get done."

He called Sophie, who was allowed to come sit in the hall with him. The receptionist tried to get them to sit in the waiting room to be more comfortable. He'd snapped at her saying he wouldn't be comfortable until he knew his wife and baby were safe. Several minutes later, Liz stuck her heard back out the door.

"Congratulations, Mr. Harrington! Looks like you are the daddy to a five pound ten-ounce baby boy." She smiled up at him. "He's nineteen inches long and has a ton of dark hair. We're sending him to the neonatal intensive care unit because he's a little on the small side and a little early, but he came out yelling like he was good and mad." She giggled. "That's always a good sign."

Joy filled his heart. It sounded like the baby was healthy, maybe just a little small. "And Lila?"

"Dr. Sullivan is working on finishing up. I will come out when I have more news."

Grant hugged Sophie again. They both were teary and smiling. "It sounds like they are both fine. Oh, thank God." Grant sat back down, bending over to rest his elbows on his knees. Adrenaline surged through causing his legs to shake. He got up, started pacing the halls. He just wanted to hear Lila was done in surgery, then he could relax.

He looked up to see Ulysses and Delores come through the door. A few minutes later, Nick and Lawrence arrived. Congratulations were said, but the celebration was postponed until Liz came back with another report. Minutes turned to an hour, and Grant started to sweat. Finally, Liz appeared at the door.

"I'm sorry, Mr. Harrington." Her face was pale and sweat clung to the side of her temples. "Lila had some complications." Grant felt the blood drain from his face. "Dr. Sullivan is doing all she can. There was bleeding in the peritoneal cavity before delivery. We're trying to find out where it is coming from and if we can stop it."

"Grant?" Delores walked up to him. "What's going on?" The family and friends gathered around him. He felt as if he might smother to death from the people around him. All of a sudden, he realized the truth. Nothing mattered but his baby and Lila. Nothing. If he lost her...if he lost her...He was vaguely aware of his father guiding him to a chair. He somehow recanted the words to them, then watched as one of the most powerful men in Washington sobbed.

27

Lila woke up groggy. Her mouth felt like cotton. Scenes from the night before flashed in her mind. Grant was crumpled up on the tiny couch. He stirred and opened his eyes to see her looking at him, confused. Her hand drifted down to her tender abdomen. *The baby. Oh God, my baby.*

She wasn't sure if she actually uttered the words out loud, or if Grant could just tell by the look on her face. He jumped up off the bed and was at her side in an instant. "The baby is going to be alright, Lila. He's in the NICU. The doctor said he's going to have to stay for a few days to be monitored and get a little bigger." He grabbed her hand. "I've never been so scared in all my life."

She reached for him, pulling is head close to hers. She felt the stubble from his cheek brush hers. She ran a hand through his soft hair, kissed him gently.

"I decided on a name. I think I'd like to call him Hudson Grant Harrington, if that's okay with you."

Grant wrapped his arms around her, squeezing her tightly. "I love that name," he murmured into her ear. She yelped as his bear hug put pressure on her abdomen. "I'm sorry. How are you feeling?"

"Sore. Very sore. I want a shower."

"Let me buzz the nurse and see if it's ok for you to get up." He didn't hear the door open.

"I'll help her shower." Delores breezed in with coffee, sodas, and snacks. Ulysses was carrying the largest bouquet of roses Lila had ever seen.

"Mom? Dad?" She remembered her conversation with Sophie and knew that it needed to occur. Just not then. It surprised her how glad she was to see her parents. She hugged them both tightly."

"Let's kick these men out, and I will help you with your shower. We can get the nurse to help us with the IV."

Lila glanced at her arm. "Why am I..." She tried to remember but couldn't. "Why do I have all these things on me?" She fingered one of the wires hooked to her chest and leading to a big monitor. Grant filled her in on the events of the night before.

There was a knock on the door. A nurse followed by Sophie walked in. "Mrs. Harrington! So good to see you awake. I'm Liz. I'll be taking care of you."

"It's nice to meet you." She tried to sit up, but the incision made it almost impossible for her to bend. She braced against Grant's arm, pushing herself up. Sophie hugged her, kissing her cheek. Lila turned to Liz. "Can I take a shower now?"

"Probably need to wait until tomorrow. You're still pretty fresh out of surgery, and we want to make sure you are feeling up to it. I can help you with a sponge bath and get you in some fresh clothes." *Clothes.*

"Oh, I didn't even...we'll we just kinda panicked...."

Sophie jumped up. "I can get you some clothes. I'll go get them now if you want."

"I have a bag packed and ready to go. It's in my closet. A big blue and green bag. Is there anyone else who could get it for us? I want you to stay."

"I'll send Nick for it. He's got a spare key anyway."

She sat back slowly. The thought of having her own things made her feel better. "Liz, what about the baby? I want to see him."

"He's doing well, ma'am. He came out crying and fussing, not too excited about being brought into this world so early. He's thriving though. He's already tolerated a small feeding by mouth."

"He's already eating?" The tears that threatened to fall before, now slipped out. "I can't believe I'm not feeding him his first bottle. I thought I might breast feed but wasn't sure."

"There's still plenty of time for that." Liz smiled. "We go ahead and try to get the baby to tolerate a first feeding so that his blood sugar doesn't get too low after delivery."

Lila absorbed this information. *Makes sense.* She calmed down some but still felt anxious and overwhelmed. "When can I see him?"

"We can go now if you like. Or we can wait after your bath?"

"No, I want to go now. I can't wait to see Hudson." *Hudson.* It was her name, a name she'd said a thousand times, but it sounded completely foreign to her ears using it in reference to her child.

"Let me get a wheelchair then we can go." A few moments later, Liz returned with a bulky wheelchair. Lila was nervously about all the cords that seemed to be coming from her, but Liz expertly unhooked cords and positioned her IV pole so that it was convenient to roll beside her on the way down to the NICU.

As they went down the long corridor to the NICU, the sharp scent of disinfectant, alcohol, and freshly waxed floors met her nose. She realized she wasn't nauseated for the first time in forever. A huge grin spread across her face as her iron stomach returned. *Thank God.*

They approached a sign that read NEONATAL INTE-SIVE CARE UNIT in large navy block letters. Two huge steel doors stood between her and her baby. Liz swiped her badge across a small black box on the wall, and the doors magically opened. What lay behind those doors stunned Lila. It was like a small beehive of activity. Nurses walked to and fro, moving fast, as they carried various medical supplies, bottles, or even small bags that had something cream colored in them.

"What's in those bags?" she asked Liz.

"Frozen breast milk. Moms often have so much milk that we freeze it so it doesn't ruin and use it to feed the babies. Of course, each baby only gets their mother's milk, so they are labeled, just like a medication would be." Bells were constantly going off, some more just dinging sounds, others were urgent, alarming sounds. One nurse went sprinting down the hall toward a bed with one of the shrieking alarm type sound. Lila shuttered.

"Ok, here we are. You guys are at Pod 8. This is where Mr. Harrington is." *Mr. Harrington.* Like he was an old man or something.

She gasped when she saw her beautiful, small baby boy. He has a shock of dark, thick brown hair. His little nose was a perfect, turning up ever slightly at the end. Just like hers. She quickly counted ten fingers and ten toes. His eyes were shut but the lids moved involuntarily, as if he must have been dreaming.

"He's doing great." Another nurse came over and intro-duced herself, saying she would be taking care of him overnight. Later, a tall, thin doctor told her that Hudson seemed to be doing very well, and if he did well overnight, they most likely would let him discharge him from the NICU in a day or two.

She took all the information in, trying to be strong for him, but the feeling she got when she saw that little boy was just indescribable. Her whole world had changed in an instant. She knew she would never do anything to cause this little one any pain.

Grant was sweet and attentive while they sat and watched the baby in silence. She didn't want to leave him, but after about fifteen mins, Grant nudged her softly.

"Somehow your dad got somebody at a local boutique to buy you all new clothes and had them laundered." He chuckled. "Guess he does come in handy sometimes."

She looked at Hudson wistfully. She wanted to carry him upstairs with her. He wasn't supposed to be down here, hooked up to wires and cords and having bells ringing and shrieking around him constantly.

"Liz, I guess we better get back to the room and get that bath."

Liz wheeled her back up to the small hospital room. Nick waited outside, and Grant politely excused himself to talk to his friend while Delores and Liz had the job of helping her take some semblance of a bath. She was embarrassed at how her stomach looked. For some reason, she thought it would look somewhat like it had before the baby, but instead, the skin looked loose and flabby. When she mentioned this to Liz, the kind nurse assured her that this often happens and usually the skin would start to spring back on its own.

Delores chuckled. "I had stretchmarks from carrying you. It took a ton of creams and finally some laser surgery to get those things off." She ruffled Lila's hair. "Worth every penny."

When she'd gotten cleaned up, she felt much more like herself. She swiped on some lip gloss and spritzed on one of her favorite perfumes that she'd tucked into the purse. *Now, I feel more human.*

Grant came back in a few minutes after Liz left, looking sheepish. "I have to go do a media event. Reporters have been hounding Nick for more information. It will be easier this way. I want you to watch because I'm going to be on the local news here live." He picked up the remote, flipping to the right channel. "I'll be back as soon as I can, ok? Please make sure you watch it." She nodded, wondering why he cared if she watched the news, but agreeing since it seemed so important to him. He kissed her softly on the top of her head and left.

28

She dozed on and off, until she heard Grant's voice come across the television. A reporter shoved the microphone in his face, asking for details about the baby.

"I came here today to announce the truth about my marriage." She jerked forward, grabbing at her abdomen. "I met Lila Hudson at restaurant in a small inn. We didn't know each other, but I think we recognized something in each other. She had just been left at the altar, and I was trying to pull my campaign together. We bonded, spending the whole time laughing, getting to know each other, and well... forgetting about what was really going on in our lives." He paused. He looked deep into the camera. "Circumstances led us to decide that we wanted to do right by our child, so we got married. Due to the fact that we both had public lives, we created a sham story about how we met and hoped the public would buy it.

Lila could hardly breathe. *What the hell is he doing?* "We married because it was the easiest thing for us to do. We made promises to each other that we thought would benefit us both. In the end however, things happened that we didn't foresee. Or at least they did for me." He held up his left hand, the simple gold band on his left hand shining in the light of the camera.

"Lila, I hope to God you are watching. I love you. I think I loved you from the time I first met you, but now... well, now I know I truly want to spend the rest of my life loving you and loving our son. I want to raise a family with you and grow old with you. If I become senator, if I don't... it really doesn't matter if I don't have you."

Her heart trembled. *Was this real?* Did he really love her? He seemed to think for a moment before he continued. "If you don't love me, I will uphold my end of the bargain. And I will always make sure you and Hudson are taken care of. I don't want to marry you because you are the mother of my child. I want to marry you because you are the most amazing woman I've ever met. You are what I've waited and searched for." He looked deep into the camera.

"Lila, will you please ever forgive me? I lied to you and the people of our state. I lost sight of what was so important to me. I always thought I had to be someone successful to be loved. Now I know that isn't true. If you'll have me, I'll spend the rest of my life with you trying to make you happy."

He handed the mic back to the reporter, who seemed speechless. There were a few moments of awkward silent air time, before the reporter seemed to finally find his voice.

"But, ummm...Mr. Harrington? Aren't you already married to Mrs. Harrington?" The question was so innocent, so simple, that Grant burst out laughing. He was still laughing while the reporter signed off, albeit a bit perplexed.

EPILOGUE

❧

November 4, 2014

Grant cradled Hudson against his chest, as the crowded room of supporters anxiously watched the bottom of the TV screen. While the final votes were counted, he handed Hudson to Nick, then took Lila's hand. The votes were tallied, then the announcement made. Grant barely edged out Senator Henry to secure the Senate seat. The newscasters were all amazed at how one area in the state pushed the senator into victory. The photographs snapped by people who saw Grant volunteer that day in the Delta made their way around social media and secured him the votes in those poverty stricken areas.

Lila beamed at Grant and kissed him squarely on the lips. "I'm so very proud of you."

Grant grinned from ear to ear. "I love you and want you to be my wife until the day I die." He dropped to one knee.

"So, if you'll have me, I have to make it official. Will you marry me? Again? We'll go to Ireland for the wedding and honeymoon. Whatever you want."

Her heart filled with joy, as she looked at the man she'd grown to love with all her heart. "Yes, of course. Yes." Grant wrapped her in his arms, sealing their contract with a kiss.

THE END

THANK YOU!!

Thank you for reading *A Political Proposal*. I hope you enjoyed Grant and Lila's story! This is my first novel, so any feedback is welcome. The best way to help an author is leaving an honest review (good or bad) on Amazon and Goodreads. This helps other readers find my books and lets me know how you think I can improve my writing.

*Would you like to know when my next book is available? You can sign up for my newsletter at www.ecfountain.com. You can also check out my blog posts where I talk about writing, reading, and other random, fun things!

    *You can find me on Facebook at https://www.facebook.com/ecfountain. You can find me on Twitter at @ECFountain.

    Thank you so much for taking the time to read my book!

Made in the USA
Monee, IL
19 July 2021